Protecting Yanira

A Damsel In Distress Bodyguard Romance

TN Seal Security Nashville Division
Book 3

KeKe Renée

Chiquita Dennie

304 Publishing Company

Note To Readers:

Protecting Yanira is revamped from previously being published under another author world. Same story with updated characters of the original TN SEAL Security series.

Latest Releases by Keke Renée:

By Keke Renée:
Wet Heat
Every Time We Touch (A Wet Heat Novelette)
His Peace, Her Pleasure
Baby, It's Cold Outside
Love Don't Live Here Anymore (Andrew sisters) Book 1
Love Don't Live Here Anymore (Andrew sisters) Book 2
One Night Only-A Novelette
Deidra's Love
Haven
Seeking To Please
Seek To Touch
Seek To Bare
Seek To Love
Seek To Trust
Seek To Earn
Tease Me Book 1
Promise Me Book 2

Consume Me Book 3

Claim Me Book 4

Tempt Me Book 5

Ravage Me Book 6

Sensual

Protecting Bria (TN Seal Security Nashville Division Book 1)

Protecting Chanel (TN Seal Security Nashville Division Book 2)

Protecting Yanira (TN Seal Security Nashville Division Book 3)

Latest Releases By Chiquita Dennie

Series

<u>Struck in Love</u>

The Early Years-A Prequel Short Story

Ruthless:Antonio and Sabrina Book 1

Savage: Antonio and Sabrina Book 2

Beast: Antonio and Sabrina Book 3

Captivated By His Love:Janice and Carlo

Brutal: Antonio and Sabrina Booke 4

Redemption: Antonio and Sabrina Book 5

<u>Heart of Stone</u>

Broken, Book 1 (Emery & Jackson)

A Valentine's Day Short Book 1.5 Emery & Jackson

Rebirth, Book 2 (Jordan and Damon)

Reveal, Book 3 (Angela and Brent)

Bottoms Up Book 3.5 Jessica and Joseph Short

Renew, Book 4 (Jessica and Joseph)

<u>Cocky Billionaire Boys</u>

Cocky Catcher (Cocky Billionaire Boys Book 1)

Bossy Billionaire (Cocky Billionaire Boys Book 2)

<u>The Fuertes Cartel</u>

Stolen (The Fuertes Cartel Book 1)
Saved (The Fuertes Cartel Book 2)
Betrayed (The Fuertes Cartel Book 3)
<u>Carrington Cartel</u>
Torn: The Carrington Cartel Book 1
Claim: The Carrington Cartel Book 2
<u>Something</u>
Something Gained: A Romantic Comedy Book 1
Something Earned: A Romantic Comedy Book 2
<u>Pierce Motors</u>
Refuel: (Pierce Motors Book l)
Pressure: Pierce Motors Book 2)
<u>Summer Break</u>
Summer Nights: (Summer Break Book 1)
<u>TN Seal Security</u>
Aydin: Book 1
Nasir: Book 2
Nicco: Book 3
<u>Standalones</u>
Until Serena(HEA World Novel)
Temptation
She's All I Need
I Deserve His Love
Mutual Agreement
Scoring with Sadie
Exposed (A Bodyguard Novel)
Love Shorts:A Collection of Short Stories
Red Light District(A Fantasy Romance Short)

I WANT TO THANK the readers for loving these characters so much and waiting for them to return.

Disclaimer

THIS WORK OF FICTION contains strong language and explicit sexual content and is only intended for mature readers. This story may contain unconventional situations, locations, language, and sexual encounters that may offend some readers. This book is for mature readers (18+).

Introduction

Grab some wine and get ready for spicier, sinful, sexy fun with Bishop, Yanira, and the team from TN Seal Security Nashville Division.

Are you signed up for my newsletter?

Join today and find out all the latest in new releases, contests, giveaways, sneak peeks, and more.

Synopsis

Investigating a murder put her in danger, but can she ignore the attraction to the man who vows to protect her?

Yanira

The last thing I expected when I turned in my story was to find myself in the middle of a murder. When I'm assigned a bodyguard, I wasn't prepared to go toe-to-toe with the man. As a journalist I have to remain objective, but I have opinions and suspicions of my own. I'm determined to find out what's going on, even if my new, sexy bodyguard would prefer I let others handle it.

Bishop

A night of blowing off steam with my friends quickly changes course when a feisty woman lands in my arms. From the moment I lay eyes on her I'm certain of two things. One, she's in grave danger, and two, she's as irresistible as she is bossy. I'm trained to defend and protect, but no one trained me how to handle a woman like her.

Will Bishop and Yanira be able to find the killer before

he finds her? Or will the sexual tension compromise their search?

Grab your copy of Protecting Yanira now and indulge in a romantic suspense unlike anything you've ever read. If you enjoy military romances, damsels in distress, forced proximity, and steamy romance, then this is a series you don't want to miss.

Prologue:

Unknown

I smiled at my latest work. I put too much time and effort into this plan for anything to mess up what I've built.

So many years stuck in the same position because of bullshit higher-ups not letting my stories get the shine they deserved. It is laughable how they run around and push that bitch Yanira into the spotlight, but a rude awakening is coming, and I plan to make my name the biggest story the paper has ever seen.

So many years of getting pushed aside, ignored, and not having a family that loved me. I had to work extra hard, even though many people forgot about me, except for one person who always had my back.

My stomach growled as I continued to stir cream in the coffee.

Today I'd planned to force the editor to hear me out during our meeting. The latest rumblings were that the owner would run a story that could hurt people who have supported me. A string of issues had popped up, making headlines that had me on edge, and only one person could have planted those stories. If I could make it all disappear,

I'd be one step closer to the future I'd always wanted. My family would be surprised at how far I'd come if they hadn't thrown me away.

"You listening?" Yanira asked.

"Huh?"

"I said thanks for making the coffee this morning." Yanira held the cup to her red lips and smiled, showing off her perfect white teeth before she left the breakroom.

I gritted my teeth as she laughed at something one of the other writers said. Everybody at the newspaper was blind to her lies. It was almost impossible to get a step up in this business unless you were Yanira. I didn't fall for her fakeness and knew it was time to make the world aware of who she truly was. All it would take was one little accident, and Yanira would be out of my life for good.

I gazed at the clock on the wall and smirked at how the steps I put in place were slowly panning out in my favor. Not in a hurry, I carried my cup and went to hear the latest gossip and read over my notes before the conference call.

Chapter 1

Yanira

Friday night

"You work too late, Nira," Mom fussed.

I rubbed my eyes, then pushed a pen into the middle of my bun and shoved my glasses up my nose. "Mom, it's not even eleven pm." I chuckled and tossed a piece of crumpled paper in the trash can. Long hours were expected for reporters, and my mother complained even though I'd been doing this for years.

Mom sighed and muttered, "You know I worry."

I lifted my gaze from the computer screen. "Why are you up so late?"

"Your brother needed someone to watch Artemis Jr."

"Where did he fly to now?"

I grew up in a family where everyone knew what the others were doing thanks to our family chat thread. My brother was a doctor and had taken his wife on vacation, but I figured they were back in town now. Artemis was older at thirty-seven, and we were close. Growing up our parents instilled in us to have each other's backs no matter what was happening in the world.

"He took Naarah to New York for a two-day visit," Mom replied, and I heard a door click.

"Are you checking the locks?"

Edda and Ozzy Thornton lived a modest life. When my brother left the Navy and became a doctor, he offered to buy them a bigger house, but they wanted to stay in the home we grew up in.

"Always. When are you leaving?"

I swung my head lazily to the other side of the office and checked the clock on the wall. "Soon. I have a few more things to type up."

"All right, little girl. Don't be too late."

I stretched out my arms, then flipped through the piles of papers on my desk. "I promise, old lady."

"This old lady can still get down," Mom teased.

I glanced out the window. There was loud music from the club across the street. I rose up to see the crowd move in and out of the door. Shaking my head, I sat down and tossed my half-eaten sandwich in the trash.

The chocolate almond butter smoothie I brought to work was nearly gone as I closed my eyes. "Goodnight, Mom. I'll call you tomorrow."

"Goodnight. Don't stay there too late."

Her overprotectiveness made me smile, so I disconnected the call. Sliding my cell into my purse, I crossed my legs and stared at the story on the screen.

After researching for a few weeks and interviewing some tenants, I found out the mayor was taking bribes. It was on its way to being the best work I'd ever published at *The Washington Tribune*.

My eyes were weary from looking at the screen for so long. It was another night of me being here alone. It was almost ten at night, and usually, I left around midnight. The noise from the club adjacent to our building was annoying. It was nonstop, with cars driving up and down the street, drunk women and men fighting, and trash on the street every morning.

I typed the final touches on the mayor's expose, hit save, and printed a copy. I moved to my email and sent a backup of the story to myself. I shut down the computer, grabbed my purse, and packed my things to leave.

I dropped the empty cup in the trash, grabbed my coat off the rack, and slid my arms into each sleeve. Closing my door, I glanced around the empty cubicles in the office. I sighed—another night of working rather than hanging out with my friends. The editor-in-chief was an asshole and hated it when I challenged him on the direction of my stories. I knew what I wanted to convey, and he couldn't get behind me bringing up these issues because he was friends with the mayor. But he needed to be told, and I didn't fall in line like every other writer on staff.

As I trekked down the corridor, I noticed the chief's lamp was on. He usually left around six or seven. "I'm shocked," I muttered, holding the story tightly in my hand.

I knocked on the door with no response. After knocking again, I pushed the door slowly.

My mouth fell open in shock at the sight that greeted me. "Everett?"

I dropped the papers on the floor before rushing toward his body and checking for a pulse.

"Oh, my God, he's dead."

A letter opener protruded from his back and blood was splattered around the room.

"I need to call the police." I reached for the phone and paused. It would be best to use my cell back in my office. I knew from reports that fingerprints could be picked up.

I raced from the office and down the hall, peering at my office. I froze when I saw my door half-open. I knew I shut and locked it behind me before leaving. Cautiously, I moved to see who was inside. My foot caught on something, which fell with a thump. I cursed under my breath as I looked down at the trash can.

The ruffling in my office stopped, which caused me to back up. Heart thumping, I ran toward the elevators and banged on the call button for security. I hit the button for the doors again, and, as I looked back to the hallway, I saw a shadowy figure dressed in black.

I screamed as a bullet hit the wall and exploded next to my head. I dropped to the ground and scooted toward the exit stairs as another gunshot exploded behind me. I shoved the exit doors open then sprinted down the ten flights of stairs from my office. I heard the door open above me, and a third gunshot rang out.

"Shit!"

My breath was ragged and my chest pounded as sweat dripped down my face. My anxiety increased as I remembered my purse was in the chief's office.

Finally, I made it to the exit and pushed open the door. I surged forward and ran into the alley, turned left, and crashed into a hard body.

I screamed, scratched, and struggled in his grip. "Let me go!"

My brother always taught me to leave a mark on the person that tried to hurt me.

"Hey, calm down," a deep, gruff voice commanded.

I tried to shove him away, but his grip only got tighter. "You're trying to kill me! Help! Let me go!"

"Who's after you?" He finally released me.

I shook my head, wiped my tears, and looked behind me. "My boss. He's..."

The man's brow hiked. "He's what?"

"He's dead." The realization hit me like a ton of bricks.

He moved me to the side. "Wait here."

I gripped his arm. "No! You can't. They have guns."

He stared at me for a moment before nodding. "Where do you work?"

"The newspaper. *Washington Tribune.*"

"Yo, Bishop, you forgot your wallet." A tall, muscular guy approached, his brows furrowed as he looked at the man he'd called Bishop, along with another man next to him. "What's going on?"

Bishop gazed at me. "I don't know. She ran from the alley and said her boss is dead."

The man handed Bishop his wallet. "Are you sure?"

I nodded, and Bishop walked toward the alley. "Wait. I should call the police."

"Whoever's in the alley should be afraid of Bishop," the tall man remarked as Bishop disappeared. "I'm Maddux, and that's Bishop and Soaquan." He held a hand out for me to shake.

I hesitated before I shook it. "Um, Yanira."

Soaquan chucked his head up at me.

Bishop came back around the alleyway as two police cars arrived. The officers jumped out and headed into the building.

"Did you call the police?" I questioned, surprised they got here so quickly.

Bishop removed his phone and texted. "No, but maybe somebody in the building did."

"Oh."

"I didn't see anyone in the alley. Are you sure someone followed you?" Bishop asked as he finished his text.

Before I could reply, an ambulance approached, and paramedics headed inside the building. A second later, another car pulled up, and Otto, the security guard supervisor, jumped out, making a beeline for me. "Yanira, did you hear?"

I nodded and hugged myself. "Everett is dead."

Otto thrust his jaw forward. "Who called you?"

I bit my bottom lip. "I found him." I closed my eyes and recalled the terrible vision of him slumped over his desk.

Otto's eyes widened. "Damn." He turned to the two men by my side. "Who are you?"

"This is Maddux and Bishop. I ran into them after someone shot at me."

Otto's head jerked back in confusion. "Wait. Shot at you?"

The paramedics came out of the building as the news outlets arrived.

"You might be the last person who saw him," Maddux pointed out.

I shook my head, trying to absorb everything. "I left my purse."

"In your office?" Otto asked.

"No, Everett's office. I ran out and went to my office." I still hadn't made sense of things.

A muscle ticked in Otto's jaw. "And what happened?"

"Otto!" another guard shouted.

"I shut and locked my door, but when I returned, it was slightly open." The night air became colder and cars blasted their horns.

Bishop's gaze narrowed on me. "Are you sure you locked it behind you?"

"I'm positive. What if whoever did this has my address?"

"Otto! The police want to talk," the guard called again.

Otto sighed and rubbed a hand down his face. "Yanira, stay here, and I'll get a police officer to escort you home."

"I can take her home," Bishop volunteered.

I shook my head. "I can take myself."

The police approached us. "Otto, we need a list of everyone who works here."

Otto gestured to me. "This is Yanira Thornton. She worked late tonight and discovered the body."

The officer turned to me. "I'm Officer Owen," he said, pulling out his notepad and pen and scribbling my name. "What can you tell us about tonight, Yanira?"

Flashes of light blinded me. I covered my eyes and backed up as cameras were pushed in my face.

"Can you tell us what happened here tonight!" a reporter questioned.

"Hey, back up!" Officer Owen shouted, waving his hands at the crowd.

"Can she come down to the station tomorrow?" Bishop suggested to the officer.

Office Owen frowned. "Who are you?"

"Bishop!"

Everyone turned at the sound of Bishop's name.

"I was waiting for y'all to come back to the bar." Another muscular man with a low-cut fade jumped into the situation. He looked like a Greek god.

"Can I come by tomorrow? It's been a lot," I said with a weary sigh.

Officer Owen closed his notepad and put his pen in his front pocket. "Come as soon as you can tomorrow." He pulled two business cards out of his pocket and handed one to Bishop and me.

"Thank you."

Otto rubbed my arm in comfort, then pulled me in for a hug. "Are you sure you're fine?" Otto had been a great friend. We'd gone to lunch together a few times.

I gave him a quick hug. "I'm fine, I promise."

"Bishop, right?" Otto reached his hand out, and they shook.

The tall man who knew Bishop and Maddux frowned. "What did I miss?"

"Cairo, this is Yanira. She discovered her boss dead," Bishop explained.

"Did you call the guys?" Cairo inquired. All three of them left me speechless with their broad shoulders, chiseled jawlines, and muscular build.

Bishop pointed around the corner. "She said she was being chased from the alley."

"We can drop her off," Maddux suggested.

Bishop narrowed his eyes at Maddux. "I'll drop her off."

I looked between them. "I can call my friend to pick me up," I insisted. I reached for my cell and remembered it was in my purse. "Shit!"

Bishop's mouth thinned. "What is it?"

"My phone is in my purse." I groaned, planting my hands on my hips.

"Bishop and Soaquan will drop you off. I'll look into what happened with your boss," Cairo told me.

"How? Are you the police?" They weren't in uniform unless they were off duty.

"No, we're security. Ex-Navy SEAL," Bishop said, removing his keys from his pocket.

My eyes widened. "My brother was in the Navy."

"Good for him." Bishop walked toward his car.

"What's his name?" Cairo asked, following him.

"Artemis Thornton."

All eyes snapped to me like I'd said something wrong. My brother had told a few stories of his time, but nothing concerning issues with his team members.

"Doc Thornton is your brother?" Cairo shook his head and chuckled.

I smiled as I thought of my older brother being a pain in the ass when I was younger. "Yes. He's out of town with his wife."

"I haven't seen Artemis since I moved back to the city," Maddux commented, brushing a hand down his cheek. His dimples would have any woman begging for his time.

"You worked together?" I asked eagerly.

"We all worked with him," Maddux responded.

Bishop cocked his chin up. "Are you coming?" he called from a Jeep.

"He's pleasant," I said wryly.

Cairo handed me his business card. "I'll be in touch. And tell Artemis to call me." Cairo came across like a protective brother.

I nodded, flipping the card back and forth. "I will."

"Cairo, call me tomorrow. The mayor called about a job," Bishop said.

I strolled toward the Jeep and climbed into the passenger seat. Bishop closed the door and Soaquan sat in the back, focusing on his phone while Bishop flipped on the lights and fastened his seatbelt.

"What did the mayor want?" Soaquan asked.

Bishop started the car. "We can talk about it tomorrow."

Hearing the mayor's name reminded me of my story.

The car started to pull into the lane, and I grasped Bishop's arm. "Stop!"

He hit the brakes. "What the fuck?"

"I need to get my bag from upstairs." I could tell from his glare that he regretted the offer to take me home.

I hopped out as they yelled for me to wait.

"She's going to get herself killed," Bishop fussed as he put the car in park.

Chapter 2

Bishop

An hour before the incident.

I slammed the beer on the table and clapped Soaquan on the back as he stared at the waitress sauntering by in shorts and a tank top. They'd been flirting all night, and my boy had no luck with our bet on getting her number.

A band played on the stage, and we ordered a round of drinks and reminisced about our time in the service. Aydin came out to help us celebrate the opening of the offices here in Downtown Nashville with my company. I ran a private firm that handled politicians and businesspeople. One of our clients was the mayor, and he'd recommended us to a real estate entrepreneur worth over a billion dollars.

I held out my hand and grinned. "Pay up." My dream of having a business on the side while still working with Cairo meant a lot, and he never once tried to force me out.

Soaquan flipped his wrist, checked the time, and gulped down his beer. "Fuck you. I still have thirty minutes."

I chuckled. "Cairo, what did we say?"

"He's right, Soaquan. You lost this one," Cairo insisted.

Maddux clapped Soaquan on the shoulder and pulled out his phone as it rang. The only person who would be calling is Chanel since she was home with the kids.

I laughed as the waitress slid next to Cairo and whispered in his ear. She was wasting her time. Cairo was head over heels in love with Bria.

"Where's Aydin?" I looked around the crowd.

"Bathroom," Cairo replied.

I lifted the beer bottle to take a sip when my phone rang. I stared at my cell and saw it was the mayor. I held my hand up for the guys to give me a second. "I need to take this."

Soaquan popped the top on another beer. "If it's one of your girls, see if they'll bring a friend." He winked at the waitress as she took the empty bottles.

I eased out of my chair. "It's the mayor." I headed to the bar's back door and stepped into the alley. "Mr. Keller, it's a little late to be calling."

"Bishop, I know it's late, but I have a meeting tomorrow at the last minute."

I gritted my teeth, annoyed to be given last minute details. "What time? My assistant can schedule those." It was almost 10 pm, and I rarely took calls this late unless it was an emergency.

"This one needs a little discretion."

Soren Keller was a typical politician who played it up for the camera, kissed babies, and showed his face when a disaster occurred. But he was back to his egotistical, selfish ways once the camera shut off.

"Send me the details."

"Sounds good. I'll text them over."

I grunted and ended the call. Stretching my tight neck muscles, I paced the alley and waited for his message.

I bumped into someone and dropped my phone. "Fuck!" I reached down to pick it up before either of us stepped on it and remembered the guys would come out soon.

"Let me go!" she screamed and tried to claw my eyes out.

"Hey, calm down!" Whatever she was running from really scared her because her fight to get free increased.

The memory of earlier played in my mind as I watched Yanira continue to complain after security pulled her back to the car.

"The police have the whole place locked down."

"I can tell them I work there," Yanira argued, pressing her plump lips into a straight line.

"Not tonight. Where do your parents live?" I had to focus on the road before we ended up in an accident. It was too dark in the alley to see her face, but when the light came on in the car I could see the strikingly beautiful woman.

"My parents live in Goodlettsville, but you can drop me off at my best friend's."

"Where is that?" A possessiveness crept through when she poked her lip out and crossed her arms.

Her deep brown eyes stared back at me. "Brentwood."

I drove through downtown and hopped on the freeway. As the streetlights beamed through I took in Yanira's full appearance, her dark bronze skin, and warm orange-red undertones. I looked in the rearview mirror, and Soaquan smirked. I wanted to flip him off but didn't want to draw her attention.

Turning off the freeway, I arrived and parked at her friend's place.

Yanira opened the door and stepped one foot out. "Thanks."

I caught her arm. "If you need help getting your things back from the police, I can make a call."

She stared at me and I removed my hand. It became clear that tonight's events had her guard up. I rarely got involved in situations with the police, but as she was the sister of one of my oldest friends, I thought I'd offer a helping hand.

Yanira looked around the area nervously. "Um, thanks. I can handle it from here."

"I thought I'd offer."

"Men usually offer if they want something in return." She slammed the door shut.

Soaquan laughed.

I flipped him off. "Fuck you." He climbed out and got in the front seat.

Soaquan shut the door behind him and got comfortable. "Bro, you're not leaving with a number tonight either."

"I wasn't looking to get her number." Our worlds were too different, we'd constantly clash. She didn't think I saw her face twist when the mayor's name came up.

As she casually walked through the parked cars I waited for her to get through the doors of the building before I drove away.

Soaquan slipped his phone in his jacket. "She's cute."

I shrugged, gazing at the side mirror for any oncoming cars.

"You don't think she's cute?" There was a critical note to his voice.

I sighed and hit the gas pedal. "I'm not having this conversation with you. Where am I dropping you?"

"Lisa's house. She got a new waterbed."

While the rest of the team was either married, or in relationships, Soaquan was out here trying to be the next Hugh Hefner and wanted me to join the club. "You're going to end up at the clinic again."

"Don't put that bad mojo on me." Soaquan checked himself out in the mirror.

"I need you in the morning for backup."

"Huh?"

My tongue was heavy with sarcasm. "To coordinate with Mayor Keller's bullshit." I parked in front of Lisa's house near the Glencoe suburbs.

Soaquan removed his seatbelt, and we shook hands. "Sure, yeah, of course."

"Call me in the morning."

"I gotcha." Soaquan shut the door.

I watched him jog up the stairs and chuckled as I drove off. "Ten bucks says they'll break up again."

Soon as he made it in I headed out of his area and sped home to Autum Creek.

I turned off the house alarm and stepped inside living room. I removed my jacket and tossed it on the counter, then dropped the keys on top of the fridge before reaching for a bottle of water.

My phone vibrated in my pocket, and I glanced at the clock on the wall to see it was past midnight. Cairo's name scrolled across the screen. "What's up?"

"Aydin wants to meet tomorrow."

Mixed feelings surged through me. "Why?"

"The killing of the editor might not be simple."

My brain was in turmoil. "What do you mean?" I leaned against the island.

"I can't talk about it over the phone. Hit me up after your meeting with Keller." Cairo ended the call.

* * *

The next morning, I stood outside with my earpiece as Mayor Keller gave a speech at a local senior center he'd used his influence to open. The crowd listened and clapped at the right moments as the media took photos and videos.

Soaquan's dark eyes showed the tortured dullness of disbelief as his voice reached me from his mic. "How much longer is this going to be?"

"Probably thirty minutes or an hour."

Soaquan rubbed a hand across his chin.

Mayor Keller stood at the podium. "As we open the first Senior Sun Rising Center, I want the families to know that the people who work here are highly qualified and skilled."

The crowd clapped and cheered at his words. I continued to scan up and down the street.

"Mr. Mayor, how many of these locations will be opened?" a reporter questioned.

"We're closing on five locations after this one," Mayor Keller answered.

"How are they being funded?" another reporter asked.

Mayor Keller lifted a cup of water and sipped. "Taxpayer money won't be used."

"That's enough for today, everyone!" the mayor's assistant called.

She escorted the mayor from the podium. I angled to stand beside him, and Soaquan was in the front. The mayor went next to the owners and shook hands as pictures were taken. A few minutes later, he loosened his tie, and we walked to the black bulletproof SUV owned by the city. Soaquan held the door open, and the mayor climbed inside, followed by his assistant and me. Soaquan took the passenger seat, and the driver took off.

He slammed his hand on the seat. "Who does that bitch think she is?" Mayor Keller growled, yanking off his tie.

"We can take her off the roster of your events list," his assistant placated.

Mayor Keller tossed his hand in the air. "Ruth, I want the entire network banned for six months."

Ruth paused and cleared her throat before speaking. "Sir, I think that would be a little extreme."

"She needs to learn a lesson," Mayor Keller grumbled.

"Yes, sir, but that would raise issues if they reported on not being allowed to attend events," Ruth explained, scrolling through her iPad.

Keller's eyes shot to me. "What do you think, Bishop?"

I pulled my gaze from the window as we drove through downtown Chicago. "I'm not the best person to answer that question, Mayor."

He waved his hand. "Come on. You saw how she tried to bait me."

I shrugged. "She was doing her job."

Mayor Keller grazed a hand down his suit jacket and blew out an exasperated breath. "She's a bitch."

We arrived at City Hall, and I stepped out, scanning the area from left to right before opening the door for the mayor to slide out. A group of protestors ran over from across the street, and I stood in front of the mayor.

"Mr. Mayor, what will you do about the housing problems?"

A young man held a sign to re-elect Mayor Keller.

Mayor Keller waved him off and continued toward the entrance. I fell into step behind him and watched as my men kept the protestors away.

"I fucking hate protestors, but they're good for business," Keller fussed.

Ruth nodded and handed him some documents to sign.

"We only have a few calls today and then some budget meetings."

He entered his office, and I stood outside for a few moments before switching with another team member.

"Are you leaving, Bishop?" Keller stood in front of his desk.

"I stationed my men around the building. You're covered."

Keller flipped through papers dropped on top of his desk. "You know we could pay you more if you worked permanently with the city."

When Cairo asked me if I was sure of opening my side business, he had some concerns with me doing too much. "I like being in control of my schedule, Mr. Mayor."

"I forgot you play by the rules." Keller chuckled.

I bit my tongue on my reply. If people knew the real man, they'd think twice about voting for him. Saved by the vibration of my phone, I reached into my pocket. "What's up, Aydin?"

"Where are you?" Aydin inquired.

"Leaving the mayor's office now."

"I'm at your office if you can swing over," Aydin said.

After waving goodbye to a few security people I knew, I slipped out the door. "Is something wrong?"

"I'd rather not talk over the phone." Something must have happened since Cairo called me last night. Aydin hated to be away from his wife for too long and he'd already been here to help Cairo and Maddux with cases.

"I'll be there in less than ten minutes." I jogged down the stairs of City Hall and hopped in the car with Soaquan.

"You talk to Aydin?" I asked.

"He just messaged me," Soaquan replied.

"I wonder what the emergency is." A muggy dampness permeated the air.

Soaquan shrugged and drove into the next lane. "Any word from that woman from last night?"

I shook my head. "Nope, not expecting anything." I scrolled through my email for upcoming meetings with new clients.

"Sounds like you're disappointed."

I pointed at the red light he drove through. "Sounds like you should be worried about not getting a ticket."

He grinned and turned up the radio. A few minutes later, we pulled up to our office and parked. I climbed out and stalked inside to see most of my friends from Aydin's team sitting around. I hadn't seen the guys in a few months.

Maddux stood at the front desk talking to our secretary, and I clapped him on the back. "Maddux, what are you doing here?"

He turned and grinned. "Brother Bishop! You know when Aydin calls, we all come." He held his hand out for a shake. Being a father and recently married Maddux hadn't come out of his bubble for a while.

I looked over at Columbo. I was surprised he'd come this time. "I never thought you'd leave Memphis," I joked.

"Normally I wouldn't, but business calls," Columbo responded as we shook hands.

"Bishop, let's talk in your office." Aydin stood at my office door. The loud laughter from the water cooler came from my best friend Rye who worked for Cairo part time when he wasn't doing work for me.

Rye followed, and we headed inside.

I slapped hands with him, clapped him on the back, dropped down in my seat, and watched the rest of the men come inside. Aydin and Cairo stood as Rye and Soaquan sat in front of me. Aydin scrolled on his phone then handed it to Cairo as they discussed something.

"Everything we say here is between us until we know we can trust people outside of the team," Aydin explained.

Whatever he was going to talk about must be worse than we expected, and it would probably put more stress on my team.

Chapter 3

Yanira

The gross smell from that day still lingered in my mind, and I was afraid to fall asleep because I'd have to see Everett's dead body again. I slid out of the bedroom and headed to the kitchen.

My best friend was at the table as she typed on her computer. "Coffee is in the pot."

I ran a hand through my hair and yawned. "Thanks."

"How are you feeling?"

As my stomach growled, I thought of what I could eat fast. "Not good." I picked up the coffee cup next to the pot and poured half a cup.

She cocked her head to the side and cupped her cheek. "Are you going to the police station today?"

"Yeah, I need an escort to return to my apartment."

Farrah Clemons was a librarian and my longtime bestie from high school and college. We'd always had each other's backs. I was there for her when she went through a divorce, and she's seen me at my lowest moments, like right now.

"Do you need me to go with you?"

I picked up a piece of bacon from the stove and sat

across from her at the table. Her marriage ended because they were both too young, and neither wanted to hold the other back. They still talked once in a blue moon, but she was more open to dating than I was. Farrah had baby doll features, big round eyes, high arched brows, and long curly hair that she tamed with Amara Beauty products from her favorite organic online store. Her height matched mine, and she had a sandy brown skin tone.

I lifted the cup to my lips. "I should be fine. What are you working on?"

"Nothing major. You're the one with the big problems." Farrah closed her laptop.

I was still in shock. "It doesn't feel real."

Farrah circled her arms around me. "You should take it easy today."

The phone rang, and she picked it up. "Hello? Yeah, she's here." Farrah passed me the phone.

"Hello?"

"Yanira, it's Officer Owen," he said.

I settled a little. "Yes, Officer Owen. I remember you."

"Good. I wanted to see if you could come to the station for some questions."

A heaviness centered in my chest. "Um, yes, I can. I wanted to ask if I could have an escort to my place."

"We can take care of that. Do you need a car to pick you up?" he offered.

I brought the cup to my lips and sipped. "No, my best friend can drop me off."

"All right. I'll see you soon." Officer Owen ended the call.

Farrah looked worried. "What was that about?"

"He wants me to answer some questions."

Farrah stood from the table. "I can drop you off on my

way to work." Farrah picked up her computer and coffee mug, sauntered to the kitchen, and placed the cup in the sink.

I crossed my legs and followed her with my eyes. "Thanks, if it's not too much trouble." In life people said family is who you counted on and I believed that, but our friendship was one of those things I would never take for granted.

"No, silly." Farrah hugged me. "It'll be fine."

"I just want this nightmare to be over."

* * *

A team of officers held the front door of the police station open as we entered, and I thanked them before strolling to the front desk.

"Hello, what can I help you with?" the front desk clerk asked.

I clasped my hands together and leaned my elbows on the counter. "I have an appointment with Officer Owen."

"You're from the newspaper, right?"

When I became a reporter my job was to not become the story and somehow in one night it changed. "How—" I scanned over his badge to check his name.

"It's all over the news. Come around to the back." He motioned to the door, as a few officers stared at us.

"I write the news, but I never expected to *be* the news."

Officer Grady gestured over his shoulder. "His office is down the hall to the left."

I looked passed him and watched as people came in and out of different rooms. "Thank you, Officer Grady." I found Officer Owen's door and knocked.

"It's open!" Owen yelled.

I pushed the door open and was surprised to see Bishop, Cairo, and another man there. "What's going on?"

Owen pointed to the chair in front of his desk. "Yanira, thanks for coming. You can have a seat." He motioned to the guys in the room. "You remember Bishop and Cairo from last night?"

My breath came in shallow spurts. "Yeah."

Owen pointed to the other guys. "This is Aydin, another SEAL team member."

"Nice to meet you, Yanira." Aydin extended his hand.

A knot formed in my stomach. "You, too." I sat in the chair at his desk, gripping my purse with my nerves on high alert.

"I asked you down here because we have concerns about last night," Owen informed me.

A chill carried on the silence. "What do you mean?"

"Everett was into some questionable things," Aydin spoke up.

I reared back, confused at his comment. "Like what?"

Owen flipped through a file. "We can't go into too much detail. We're still trying to put the pieces together."

"Okay, but should I be worried?"

"We think you should be under protection," Aydin said.

I chuckled. "Protection? From what?" Whatever they had going on had nothing to do with me.

"Based on what Bishop told me, I believe you're being targeted," Owen explained.

I jumped out of my seat. "Targeted? I haven't done anything wrong."

"Please sit, Mrs. Thornton," Aydin said.

My stomach churned. "Miss."

"I'm sorry. Miss Thornton." Aydin smiled.

My chest felt like it would burst. "Get to the point because I have a life, career, and family."

"For the time being, you'll be under Bishop's protection until we can find the killer," Owen demanded, passing a file to Aydin.

I looked behind me at the guy standing against the wall with his hands crossed over his chest. He didn't look too excited at the prospect of babysitting me. "Maybe you're mistaken."

Owen stood from his chair and shoved his hands in his pockets. "Whatever Everett was into got him killed, and you're a witness." Normally the cops around here hated to have outside parties on their investigations. I had tried many times to get information for my stories.

"This is crazy."

"Owen, we can take it from here," Bishop said.

My head whipped to the side. "I'm not finished."

Bishop fixed his gaze on me. "What else is there to discuss?"

I studied his face. "How do I know I can trust you? I bumped into you in the alleyway."

A low growl accompanied the darkening of his eyes. After he dropped me off last night I figured that would be the last time I'd see any of them. Honestly, I preferred to go back to my little bubble.

Aydin shook his head. "Bishop." If Aydin had to remind his friend to relax often then it meant he blew up at the littlest things.

"I have work and a family. I can't be under a bodyguard for hours on end," I reasoned.

"You won't be," Cairo stated.

My eyes shifted to him. "Thank you." As badly as I

wanted Everett to get justice, I needed to go back to my life as a reporter and put last night away.

"Because you're moving in with him," Cairo finished.

I whipped around at his statement, eyes widened in shock. "What!" I gripped the back of the chair, the anxiety of everything came up.

All eyes focused on me, and Bishop looked miserable.

"For your protection, we think you should stay with him," Cairo explained.

I waved my hands around. "No, that's not going to happen."

"Then he'll stay at your place."

I rubbed my forehead and released a frustrated breath. "My life is not some toy you can toggle back and forth. I get to dictate what happens."

"How do we work the investigation and keep you safe?" Owen questioned.

"Put some men outside my house. Job done." I threw my hands in the air.

Aydin, Cairo, and Bishop peered at each other.

Owen nodded. "We'll play it your way for now, but the minute something gets away from us, you're staying with Bishop."

"I need to speak to my family."

Owen nodded and walked around his desk. "That's why we're doing this."

"Doing what? Uprooting my life because you think some killer is out to get me?"

Bishop pushed off the wall. "Artemis told us to monitor you." He moved toward me.

"When did you talk to my brother?"

"Early this morning," Bishop replied.

I bit my bottom lip. Artemis was always trying to play the protector. I'd told him I was an adult and could handle myself many times. "My brother means well—"

"Doesn't matter. This fell into my lap, and when it involves potential harm to a team member, we handle things ourselves," Bishop informed me.

"When does this protection start?" I exhaled, placing my purse on my shoulder.

Bishop looked at his watch, then back to me. "Now."

"All right. I need to go back to my place and to the office to get some work done."

"Are you good for now, Bishop?" Aydin asked.

"Yeah. I'll have my men stationed at the office and her place en route," Bishop responded, pulled out his cell, and sent a text.

"Yanira, please let me know if you need anything." Owen passed me his business card.

Bishop took it out of my hands and slid it into his pocket. "I'll keep you updated," Bishop answered.

The four of us left the office and walked to the front of the police station, where I saw Otto in conversation with Officer Grady.

I rushed in his direction to get some answers. "Otto! What are you doing here?" I reached out for a hug.

"Hey, Yanira. I was bringing Everett's work for Officer Owen to look at," Otto said.

I dragged a hand up and down my arm. "How is everyone at the paper?"

"Somber, but working through the news," Otto answered.

Owen stepped out of his office. "Otto, I'm ready for you." The building picked up noise which interrupted us.

"I'll catch up with you, Yanira," Otto told me, and I hugged him again.

Bishop dragged his eyes from us as he walked in the front to leave. Cairo and Aydin stayed in the back as we strolled out of the station like I was a politician or famous actress. It was weird to be in this situation because I mostly wrote about people who had to have round-the-clock security and the toll it took on their life.

Black Range Rovers were lined up out front with the middle car door open, and Bishop motioned for me to climb in the back.

"We will head to your office and then your place," Bishop said, shutting the door.

* * *

An hour later, the elevator doors opened, and all eyes fell on the men surrounding me—tall, intimidating, and wearing earpieces and guns. Not that you could see the latter unless you were up close. I didn't want around-the-clock surveillance, but I knew it was necessary to catch the killer.

"Hey, Yanira, do you have a moment?" Kirsten asked.

"Uh, yeah."

Kirsten was the temporary editor-in-chief. She worked under Everett, and I had no doubt she would one day fill his shoes, just not this soon or in this manner.

Bishop followed me into her office.

Kristen closed the door behind us and motioned to the chair. "Have a seat," she said, moving to the opposite side and sitting down.

"What's going on, Kristen?" I asked.

Kristen sat with her hands clasped together, an

unamused look on her face. "I've been talking with Otto and the higher-ups."

"Okay."

"We think you should take some time away."

I jumped up, pissed at another demand. "*What?*" It felt like everyone was in on some game I knew nothing about or was given the chance to play.

To calm me down, Kristen reached out a hand. "Not permanent, but this could bring unwanted attention."

"You're kidding, right?" Maybe I was wrong in my thoughts, but we'd clashed in the past on certain stories and had to get Everett to be the mediator. *Is she using the moment for herself?*

A sigh escaped her. "I can't imagine what you've been through, but we must keep business running."

My mouth dropped open in shock. "What am I supposed to do without my work?"

"I didn't say you couldn't work, but you need to stay away from the office until we can get a better handle on things."

I shifted my gaze from Kristen to Bishop. "Can you believe this bullcrap?"

"She's right," Bishop answered.

"Of course, you'd take her side."

"I have no reason to take her side, and you're acting like a child." Bishop's eyes bore into mine.

I blew out a frustrated breath.

"Just for a few days, and then you can come back," Kristen offered.

I had no choice. If someone was after me, it was better that I was under protection until they caught the person.

A knock at the door interrupted us and caused Bishop and I to glance at the door.

"It's open," Kristen called.

Jet peeked his head inside and held up the mail. He'd worked in the mail room for five years, and we'd hung out as a group. He'd always been genuine with me.

"I have your mail, Kristen. Hey, Yanira," Jet said, placing the stack of envelopes on her desk.

I waved at him, and he acknowledged Bishop.

"Kristen, I need to talk to you." Campbell busted through the door.

I rolled my eyes.

"Whatever it is will have to wait, Campbell," Kristen blew him off.

"This is important," he snarled.

Kristen rose from the chair and took the mail, laying it on top of her incoming pile. "Don't you see me talking to Yanira?"

Campbell finally looked at me before he returned his gaze to Kristen. "This is important." He crossed his arms over his chest.

Kristen sighed, then typed on her computer. "Fine. Yanira, can we discuss this later?"

"Will I be able to continue to work on the story I planned for Everett?" It was the biggest story of my career, and I didn't want anything to stop me from completing it.

Kristen nodded, picked up her calendar, and flipped through her schedule. "Yes but do it at home."

I walked out of her office with Bishop on my trail. Grabbing the folders I needed, I trekked out of the building. "How long do I have to be under you?"

Bishop frowned. "Huh?"

"This bodyguard situation. We don't know if whoever it was will come back."

Bishop unlocked the car door. I climbed into the passenger seat and placed my bag on my lap.

"I need to talk to Aydin first," he said as he settled in the driver's seat and slid the key in the ignition.

Surely, this wouldn't last more than a day or two?

Chapter 4

Bishop

"**W**hat the hell is going on? She's been in my house for the past week!" I clenched my teeth and balled my fists.

"Bishop, it's only been three days," Aydin corrected.

"Feels like a year," I mumbled, as I dropped into the chair next to the desk he was using while he's here.

"I spoke with Kristen, her boss, and she wants this to stay quiet. Plus, the police need our help."

I rubbed my chin. "She's driving me crazy."

He chuckled. "How so?"

"After we left her place to gather some of her things, I tried to be reasonable with giving up my guestroom."

Aydin blew out a breath and rubbed his temple. "I can already tell this didn't go as you planned."

I crossed my arms and groaned, pissed at what had become my life. "She has her things everywhere."

"For now, we have to keep her under surveillance. Have you spoken to her brother?"

"No, I need to get in touch with him and her parents."

"Well, try not to kill her until you've talked to her family."

I blew out a frustrated breath. "I hear you."

The phone rang, and he answered it. "Aydin."

I stood up to leave, and he waved a hand for me to stop.

"All right. Send me the information. Don't do anything until you hear from me."

Aydin picked up his pencil, wrote something on a piece of paper, then hung up.

I raised a brow at the frown on his face. "Important call?"

"Maybe. They have the video footage, but it's blurry." Aydin logged into the computer.

My cell phone vibrated, and I counted to ten as I saw the caller ID. "Hello?"

"When are you going to get something to eat at your place? You only have beer," Yanira grumbled.

I turned my back to Aydin and closed my eyes to gather my thoughts. "I asked you before I left if you wanted to order something."

"Look, Bishop. This will not work. I need my space."

"Don't call me again unless you're in trouble." I ended the call before Yanira could reply.

Aydin shook his head. "You're wrong." He pulled up some files.

"No, she's annoying."

Aydin folded his hands behind his head. "You better hope she's still open to helping us solve this case."

"Why wouldn't she be?"

"Maybe because you act like an ass toward her."

I waved him off and lifted my phone when it vibrated.

Painintheass: *I'm leaving; you are the most difficult man I have ever met.*

Me: *You leave my house, and I will have you arrested.*
Painintheass: *I'll stay with my parents and brother.*
Me: *Then you'll end up putting them in danger.*

"Why am I texting her back?" I clicked to dial her number.

"I was wondering when you would call her," Aydin teased, fast-forwarding the video of the street across from the alleyway and bar.

"Yes," Yanira answered.

"Where—"

Her voice message cut across me. "*Sorry, I'm away from my phone. Leave a message.*"

* * *

She gazed at me, watching as I removed my jacket and turned on the hallway light. "I can always go stay with my parents."

"Aydin said to keep you close, and camping outside your folks' place would only bring more trouble."

Yanira stood in the doorway with her arms crossed.

I opened the fridge and saw it was empty of food. The doorbell rang.

"Did you tell someone where I live?" I marched behind Yanira as she headed for the door. She smiled as she took the takeaway bags from the delivery guy and shut the door. Placing the bags on the table, she turned to grab plates from the cabinet.

"You can't have people coming to my house," I told her.

She shrugged and opened the box of steamed rice and veggies. "There's no food here."

"I could have brought something home." I slumped down in the chair next to her and grabbed the bag of ribs.

"I didn't know when you'd be home, and last time you ignored me."

I shook my head. "Aydin and I had a meeting."

She poured some of the rice and veggies onto my plate. "About me going home?"

I jumped up and grabbed a drink from the fridge. "No."

"They don't even know who's behind anything."

"Either stay here or go back to your place without protection."

My phone vibrated, and I glanced down to see a name I hadn't seen in months. "Artemis."

Yanira licked the fork clean. "That's my brother," she whispered.

I nodded.

"Tell me what's going on. My parents haven't talked to my sister, and I get a call from Aydin that you and the team have her under guard. She said someone tried to kill her."

"Let me talk to him." Yanira reached for the phone, but I turned away to continue the conversation.

"Artemis, you know me and what we do."

"We need to meet soon."

"Understood."

"Protect my sister, Bishop," Artemis demanded.

I looked at Yanira, who dropped her eyes. "With my life." I ended the call and slid the phone on the table. "We should establish some rules."

She burst into laughter. "You're not my father or my husband." Yanira ate some of her food.

"I'm here to keep you alive. It's not my choice to have you in my space."

Ignoring my statement she focused on her food and I decided to give her a few minutes alone.

I escaped to my room to shower the day away before

going over the details Aydin was supposed to email on Yanira's case. I shut the door behind me, kicked off my shoes, and slid off my pants. Whoever was trying to kill her didn't care that she was a well-known journalist. It made me even more nervous that they would do anything they could to get their point across by coming for her.

Steam filled the bathroom, and I grabbed a fresh towel from the cabinet before I stepped into the shower. Whenever I came home from a long day, I set the water temperature high to work through my aching muscles.

Recalling Yanira's emotional state in the alleyway made me suspect this was personal and not a random accident of her finding her boss dead.

Twenty minutes later, I stepped out of the bathroom with the towel in my hand.

"So are you—oh, shit!" Yanira busted into my room before I had the towel wrapped around my waist.

"Do you ever knock?" I groaned, then reached into my drawer to grab a pair of boxers and a T-shirt.

Yanira turned her back. "It was an accident," she muttered as she stomped from the room.

I ran a hand across my face and released a heavy breath.

* * *

"We've got it narrowed down," Rye said, pointing at the list of people who'd entered the building during the day.

"What about the people on this list we don't have names for?"

Aydin sat in the conference room chair, and Cairo and Maddux listened intently to the discussion. Most of the team was here to help except Columbo.

There were a lot of wives and children on my team. I

was trying to find a place in this world that didn't involve fighting in a war. The place I was in at the moment had me thinking of finding something new. All night, I'd thought of my time as a SEAL. Until Yanira banged on my door and pulled me from my dreams.

"I think we should have Columbo scan everybody's face to track them down," Aydin explained.

"Who's to say the killer didn't know where the cameras are positioned, and so they didn't get caught on camera?" Maddux wondered.

All eyes turned to me.

"I'm not putting anything past this person."

"How is Yanira?" Cairo questioned.

I shrugged.

Maddox bumped me with his elbow. "She's staying with you, right?"

"Yeah."

"You don't know how she's doing?" Cairo hounded.

"I guess she's all right besides annoying the fuck out of me."

Rye and Maddux burst into laughter.

"Only time you get like this is when your mind is running in loops," Aydin reminded me.

I tossed a ball up in the air and caught it as we talked. "Nothing going on," I grunted.

"Are you sure?" Aydin insisted.

"I'm fine. How are Bria and Chanel?"

"They're great. Are you trying to date?" Cairo probed, like he always did when we all got together. He felt being married with a family helped calm him down and gave balance in life.

Despite their jokes, I waved him off. They thought I needed to do the same but finding a woman who understood me was the hard part. "I'm only here to work the case, not have an Oprah session."

"Leave him alone," Aydin muttered.

They faced the screen ahead in the conference room and replayed the video of Yanira running out of her boss's office and down the hall to the exit door.

"Have you spoken with Artemis?" Cairo asked.

Artemis calling meant I needed to meet up with him before Yanira ran her mouth to him. "He called me and wanted to know what was going on with his sister."

"He's worried like any big brother," Aydin expressed.

"What's the next step?" Rye inquired.

"We checked with the police and the case Yanira was working on." I looked at my watch. "A lot of moving pieces, I have to confirm," I volunteered.

"I'll ride with you." Rye rose from the chair.

"Cairo and Maddux can handle the conversation with Yanira," Aydin directed.

We dispersed from the office, and I checked my phone for any messages. Yanira was up eating breakfast when I left early this morning, and I hoped we can wrap her case up soon so it doesn't become a bigger hassle.

Rye and I climbed into the car, and Rye slid the key in the ignition before backing out of the parking space.

"Who's that?" he asked as my phone buzzed.

"Otto."

"The security guard?"

I nodded and clicked to answer the phone. "Otto, what's up?"

"I thought Yanira was supposed to be under your protection?" Otto queried.

Yanira and I bumped heads, but she knew when I had a

conversation with her brother I meant my words to keep her safe. "She is."

"Then why is she down at the police station asking questions?" Otto informed.

Right as I clicked my seatbelt, I froze. "What?" I barked.

Rye stopped at the light and turned to look at me. "What's going on?"

I covered the phone with my hand and moved it from my ear. "Yanira is at the police station."

Rye hit the gas when the light turned green and sped through traffic. "Shit," he cursed as he moved in and out of lanes.

"How did she get there?" I asked. Luckily traffic wasn't too heavy so we would get there faster than normal.

"I guess she called a car service," Otto said.

I clenched my fist. Yanira was a pain in the ass, taking things into her own hands.

"She's probably fucked up the case," I spat in aggravation. She had no idea if she was being followed, and we had to stop what we were doing to save her. "Let me call you back." I hung up before Otto could say anything else.

"How did she get to the police station?" Rye asked.

"I don't know. Maybe a car service." I dialed Yanira's number, and it went straight to voicemail.

Rye honked at another car to move before they blocked us to get ahead. "Should we tell Aydin to meet us at the station?"

"No, I will handle her." I dialed Artemis's number to get him on the line.

"Bishop, this better not be bad news about my sister," Artemis spat before I could speak.

My heart rate picked up. "Have you spoken to her today?"

"No, why?"

I motioned for Rye to take a short cut through a residential area. "She took off without me or letting my team know."

"Where is she?" Artemis shouted.

"The police station."

"I haven't been in that world in a while. Do I need to take charge?"

Artemis was as badass as the rest of the team. We all trained under the best and were always ready for anything. For Yanira to cause her brother to get involved, knowing he was retired, put me in an awkward position.

Rye hopped in the next lane, sped through the stop sign and hit the highest speed as he bypassed all the traffic signs to get us to the police station.

"She's safe with me, Artemis. I promise."

"This phone call doesn't give me much confidence."

I gritted my teeth at his response. "Brother, you know me. I'd lay my life down for you and your family."

"It's my sister, Bishop. Don't fuck this up."

"I'll have her call you soon."

I ended the call, and five minutes later, we hopped out and rushed into the police station.

Chapter 5

Yanira

Once Bishop left, I jumped in the shower and replayed the vision of his naked six-pack and the thick, long dick. I was in shock for the longest time and forgot my name until he barked orders, and I ran out of the room. We were like two raging bulls under the same roof, and I needed to get back home to peace and quiet.

I called for a car service and came to the police station to get some answers on my case.

"Officer Owen is busy right now," the desk clerk explained.

"I'll wait."

"It doesn't work like that, ma'am."

"My name is Yanira, and I'm pretty sure I'm younger than you," I sassed and crossed my arms over my chest. Owen was giving me the runaround, making me more determined to handle the case alone.

"Ma'am?"

I held my hand up to stop him from going any further. His cheeks turned red in embarrassment.

"Yanira!"

That voice made me freeze. He wasn't supposed to know I was missing. It wasn't like he even wanted me at his place, and he certainly didn't seem interested in finding out who was behind trying to kill me.

"Bishop, I can explain." I took a step back.

His brows furrowed in confusion as he sauntered toward me. "How did you get here?" He cocked his head, and his piercing eyes moved from the bottom of my feet to my face.

I planted a hand on my hip. The big, bad ex-SEAL thought he could intimidate me, but I grew up with a brother in the same field. He didn't scare me. "I took a car service. Any other questions?"

Bishop looked over my shoulder at the desk clerk. "Tell Owen I need to speak with him."

"Sure, Bishop," the clerk responded.

I twisted to face him with a hard glare. "Wait a minute!"

"Ma'am?" he asked calmly.

I pointed my finger in his face. "I've been here wanting to talk to Owen, and you said he was busy. Bishop comes along, and you give in to him."

The desk clerk didn't bother to answer, throwing a look at Bishop before walking off.

"After we talk to Owen, you're going back to my place," Bishop said, and I pulled my gaze from the retreating clerk.

"No, I'm not."

"Yes, you are." He gritted his teeth.

Owen walked out of the back. "Yanira, I told you I'd get in touch when we had more information."

"I have a list of people who might be behind this." I slipped my hand into my purse to retrieve the piece of paper. I'd thought about all the stories I'd written that had caused companies to threaten me and the newspaper and listed the most likely suspects.

"Okay, this is something I can work with," Owen responded, taking the paper.

"Did you speak with Aydin about the camera footage?" Bishop inquired.

"Still running facial recognition. So far, everyone has checked out," Owen said as he folded the paper.

I looked from Bishop to Owen. "Can you include me in the updates? This is my life we're talking about."

"Come back to my office." Owen turned, and Bishop and I followed behind.

As we entered his office, my cell rang. "Hey, Ma, can I call you back?"

"What are you doing?" Mom investigated.

"Um..."

"Yanira Thornton," she hissed.

"I'll explain when I get over there."

"Fine. I'll expect you here in an hour." Mom ended the call, and I tossed my phone back in my purse.

"As I was saying, I had my team question some of your coworkers, like Campbell, another editor, and a few house-keeping people," Owen explained.

"Anything suspicious?" I probed.

"Nothing stood out. I checked everybody's background, and no one has a criminal record," Owen replied.

I sighed. "My boss wants me to work from home until they find out who is behind everything."

Owen nodded. "She's right. Bishop, I know you wanted an update, but the video from the alley only showed you guys."

Bishop focused on the monitor. "Anything from before she came out?"

"Mostly staff and delivery people."

Bishop nodded.

"Owen, let me know if you find anything. I'm ready for this to be over." I started for the door.

Bishop came up behind me and pulled out his keys. "You're going with me."

"I need to meet with my parents."

"I'll drive you."

I stopped walking to face him. "Can I get someone else to protect me? Because we're not connecting."

"Connecting?"

"Yeah. I don't like your attitude."

"I don't need you to like my attitude. Keeping you alive is my priority."

* * *

"Good to see my child knows where home is," Mom teased, holding the door open.

I stepped up and kissed her on the cheek. Inside, my brother was on the couch with my dad, who had the remote in his hand.

"Artemis! When did you get here?" I ran to hug my brother.

"Not too long ago."

Bishop stood off to the side with Rye.

"Who are they?" Mom asked.

"This is Bishop and Rye. They're friends of Artemis from the Navy," I explained and waved for them to sit down.

Artemis stood and shook hands with the guys.

"Ozzy, are you ready to eat?" Mom sauntered over to my dad and plucked my nephew from his lap. Artemis Jr.

was the only grandchild and had everybody wrapped around his little finger.

"So, what's going on, Yanira?" Dad kissed my forehead and placed his arm around my shoulder.

"I missed you and Mom." I leaned my head on his chest.

"Uh huh. What do you want?"

"Daddy, I'm serious," I whined.

"Be serious, Yanira, and tell Mom and Dad what's going on," Artemis instructed.

I rolled my eyes at him. As my older brother, I knew he took his role as my protector to heart, but I could handle a crazy stalker with the police's help—no reason to worry my parents.

"Yanira, you better start talking, baby girl." Mom held my nephew on her hip.

"Mr. and Mrs. Thornton, Yanira witnessed an incident, and she's under police protection. Well, my team and I are keeping an eye on her," Bishop explained.

"What did you witness?" Dad asked.

I gently touched my nephew's hair, and watched his little smile grow. "A murder," I mumbled under my breath.

"Murder!" Mom shrieked, and my nephew started to cry.

"Naarah, take him to the bedroom," Dad said and tugged me into a chair.

All of this became real and I hated to put my family in trouble. "I didn't want the entire family to worry," I explained.

Dad took a seat across from me. "You're my child. I will always worry." He gripped my hand.

"I understand, Dad, but things moved so fast. I didn't want to say anything until I had time to prepare you."

"Bishop, is there something we can do to help? Maybe you should go out of town, Nira," Mom suggested.

I scowled. "And run like a chicken?"

"It's called being careful," Mom fussed as she sat next to Dad.

"As long as I've been in this business, no one has run me off, and I don't plan to allow them to do it now."

"You're staying here," Dad informed me.

"Actually, she's staying at my place," Bishop spoke up.

Mom rubbed a hand over her face. "Wait, this is too much."

"You don't have to worry. I'll be fine," I promised, hugging them both.

"I knew your job would become dangerous." Dad stood in a huff.

I needed to change the subject, or my father would fuss all night about me quitting, which would never happen. "Mom, what did you cook?"

"The conversation is not over, baby girl. Come on." Mom stood, and we walked to the kitchen to gather the food for dinner.

* * *

Afterwards we pulled up to Bishop's house. I had a feeling we were about to go at it again since I'd snuck off to the police station.

"Rye, call me tomorrow, and we'll start checking out the people on Yanira's list," Bishop commanded.

"Sure, Bishop. Make sure you don't fuss at our girl," Rye joked.

"Shut up," he grumbled as he stepped out of the car and opened my door.

"Thanks," I muttered, waved goodbye to Rye, and headed for the front.

Bishop slipped key inside, unlocked the door, and waited for me to enter.

I slipped off my shoes, started toward the guest room, and then paused. "Go ahead."

He shut it behind him. "Ahead with what?" Bishop raised an eyebrow.

"Yell at me. Tell me I'm stupid."

He released a sigh. "What will that solve?"

"I don't know, but you've been quiet since the police station, and I know you want to blow up on me."

He walked to the kitchen. "No reason to blow up." The silent treatment is what I hated especially with him being nonchalant.

"Come on, Bishop. I know we aren't friends, but—"

Bishop held a bottle of water and strolled down the hallway. "It's a job. I don't need to be your friend."

"That may be true, but the silent treatment is childish."

He paused with his hand on the knob of his office. "Childish?"

"Yes."

"Go to bed, Yanira." He ignored his office and moved to his bedroom.

I trailed behind him and gripped his arm to turn him around. "Not until you yell at me."

"Woman, I'm trying to be sympathetic to what you're going through, but you're trying me." I blocked Bishop with my arm as he made to move past me. "I know I was stupid to run

off, but you haven't made me feel welcome at all."

His eyes lowered to the ground briefly, then lifted back to my face. "My business is about respect, and you're running around like someone who doesn't have a target on their back."

I stepped back. "Okay."

He looked surprised. "Okay?"

"Yeah. I will do better and listen to you from now on."

"Good, because you're grounded." He angled around me.

My mouth dropped open in shock. "*Grounded?*"

"Goodnight, Yanira." He stepped into his bedroom and shut the door.

"Bishop, I'm an adult. You can't ground me!" I knocked on his bedroom door.

"See you in the morning!" he shouted.

"This isn't over!"

Chapter 6

Bishop

"**W**ho's the first stop?"

Rye looked down at the paper. "Kristen, the acting editor-in-chief."

I looked in the rearview mirror at Yanira in the backseat with a pout on her lips. I made her get up bright and early, shower, and eat breakfast. At first, she gave me hell, but I turned on the TV at high volume, so it blasted through the bedroom. She fell out of bed, and I laughed at her wild hair and grumpy face. She hated being told what to do, but we needed to close this case before it got out of hand.

"The address is right around the corner," Rye said.

"We won't be here long," I told Yanira.

Yanira leaned back in the seat and sipped on her drink. "I could have stayed at home," she mumbled.

"And miss all the fun?" I joked.

Rye chuckled. He was the jokester of the group, but when someone kept poking at me, I gave back as good as I got.

As we parked outside Kristen's home, she emerged, a

coffee mug in one hand and a backpack in the other. Rye and I jumped out of the car.

I glanced around the neighborhood. "Kristen!" I called her name as she stood by her car.

Kristen pushed her bag up on her shoulder and glared at us. "Can I help you?"

"We need to talk to you."

Kristen looked from me to Rye, then to her neighbors that came out of their house and waved. "About?" Kristen waved back with a smile.

"Yanira."

"Not sure how I can help. I left early that day," Kristen answered.

"The case she was working on wasn't approved, correct?"

She shrugged. "As far as I know, she didn't need approval, but I could be wrong."

"Yanira said it was behind her editor's back, but she would get her sources lined up."

"Most journalists won't reveal their source."

She shifted from one foot to the other. "Can you think of anyone that would want to hurt Yanira?"

"Honestly, it could be anyone. Yanira is well-known and has a lot of enemies because of the stories she writes."

"You've never had a problem with her?" Rye probed.

Kristen's forehead wrinkled in confusion, and she placed a hand on her chest. "Am I a suspect?"

"Everyone is a suspect."

"Yanira said several people would run for editor after your boss was murdered," Rye pointed out.

"And you think I killed him to get the job?" Kristen asked in disbelief.

Rye shook his head. "I never said you killed anyone."

"Gentlemen, I would love more than anyone to have Yanira back. I didn't kill my boss or try to kill her."

"Thank you for your time," Rye said.

"Please tell Yanira the story she wanted to run is fine with me," Kristen said.

We watched as Kristen climbed into her car and drove down the street.

"Your thoughts?" Rye inquired.

I took in her house. "I don't see her as a suspect."

"I got that feeling." Rye snapped photos. He'd worked with Columbo to set up cameras and audio to gather intel.

"Maybe she'll slip up, but I think it was a man based on the evidence."

We got back in the car and headed to the next stop.

Yanira leaned forward through the middle of the seat. "What did Kristen say?"

"Not much, besides she didn't kill your boss," Rye answered.

"I could have told you that." Yanira sat back in her seat.

I eyed her as she looked out the window. "Tell me about Campbell."

"He's a reporter like me and wants to be the one who gets all the juicy stories," Yanira explained.

"Anything we should know before we see him?"

She stared at me and rolled the window down. "Like?"

"Have you had a relationship with him? Do you know any of his deep secrets?"

"Unlike you, I haven't slept my way to the top," Yanira snapped.

"Didn't say you did, but most times these situations start with a relationship," I explained.

"What he's trying to say, Yanira, is it could be a crime of

passion, like a boyfriend you dumped trying to get revenge," Rye said as he eyed me in annoyance.

Great. Yanira had everyone like putty in her hands except me.

Yanira was naive to not think it could be someone who worked at the newspaper. "Rye explained it better," she said with a smirk.

"He's nicer," I replied.

"You're an asshole," Yanira muttered.

"We're here." I cut the engine and opened the door for Yanira. We ambled inside, and I held up my badge, as did Rye.

"Hello, can I help you?" The desk receptionist smiled as we entered the building.

Yanira waved at a few people near the elevator. "Hi, Tammy. We need to see Campbell," Yanira said.

Tammy typed on her computer, then glanced at Yanira. "Uh, Yanira, I'm sorry, but you're not allowed up."

Yanira leaned on her desk with her fists balled. "You're kidding?" Yanira glowered.

"No, I can see if Campbell is free to come down here," Tammy said, picking up the phone.

Yanira moved to go behind the desk and I gripped her arm to pull her back. "This is ridiculous," Yanira argued as she paced back and forth.

Tammy shifted her eyes to me and Rye, then held up her phone. "Campbell is in a meeting. Are you able to wait?"

"How long is the meeting?" I asked.

"It's the morning staff meeting, so usually an hour or two," Yanira said unhappily.

"We'll catch him another time," I said.

Yanira frowned. "Tammy, who told you I couldn't go upstairs?"

"Kristen and the board of directors," Tammy whispered, looking over her shoulder to ensure no one was listening.

"I'm so ready for this to be over," Yanira muttered.

I held the door open as we marched out of the building and back to my car.

"How about we head to one more stop and then grab something to eat?" Rye suggested.

I wanted to get a lot more done, but the defeated look on Yanira's face gave me second thoughts, so I agreed with Rye.

I hit the gas pedal and hopped on the main road with traffic. The music was on low as we drove downtown and made it to an apartment building.

"How did you know this place?" Yanira sat up straight in surprise.

I smirked. "Like you, I have my secrets."

Yanira tried to block me. "Wait. Let me do the talking."

Aydin and the team had put in extra time, and their information had led us to this apartment.

We headed for the building, and I knocked on the door. I scanned the area, noting it was well kept with little security besides a few cameras stationed up high.

The door opened to reveal a woman. "You can leave—oh, I thought you were the food delivery."

"Valencia Keller?"

Her eyes moved from me to Yanira. "Yes." She moved in closer.

"Mayor Keller's niece?"

Yanira sighed. "I'm sorry, Valencia."

"Can we come in and talk?" I asked.

Valencia looked annoyed and tried to shut the door, but

I blocked it with my hand. Valencia stepped to the side. "Fine, but I don't have to answer any questions." She closed the door behind us and motioned for us to sit on the couch.

"You've been passing information to Yanira about Mayor Keller."

Valencia glanced from me to Yanira and folded her arms over her chest. "You seem to have all the answers."

Yanira turned to me. "Bishop, the story I was working on dealt with issues about buildings that Keller owns."

"I want to know why Keller's niece is talking to the press."

"Because she understands what her uncle did was wrong," Yanira pleaded.

Valencia piped up, "Yanira, it's fine. You don't have to speak for me."

Rye and I exchanged a look. There was something fishy about Valencia.

"He's always been corrupt, and I had information on him because of my work in the mayor's office."

"What's in it for you?" I asked.

Valencia answered, "Nothing."

"I've never paid a source for information," Yanira said.

"Yanira came after me. I didn't look for her."

"How did you two meet?"

"At one of my uncle's events."

I'd watched her since we knocked on the door, and it was clear she was in this for something. Keller was underhanded and out for himself. Working as his security over the years wasn't my choice, but we kept our promise to protect people at all costs.

"The story Yanira pushed for came with inside information on the apartments and tenants," Valencia said.

"I crossed references from what she told me and confirmed with a few tenants," Yanira added.

"It wouldn't look good if it got out that the source was the mayor's niece," I noted.

Valencia's head dropped.

Yanira jumped up to cover for Valencia. "The only people who know are you and me."

A sudden crash from outside caused all eyes to turn to the window. I hurried to push the blinds back and saw a car drive off quickly.

"What's wrong?" Yanira asked.

"We need to get out of here."

Valencia rose from the couch and looked out the window. Rye and I jogged outside to find the windows of our car smashed and the tires flat.

"Someone wanted to prevent us from coming here." Rye stooped to pick up a rock sitting next to the car.

"Aydin needs to be updated." I slammed my hand on the car's roof and reached for my phone.

Yanira stood with Valencia, taking in the scene.

"Hello," Aydin answered.

"I might need some extra eyes on this case."

"What happened?" Aydin checked.

"Seems like I'm being followed."

"Where's Yanira?" Cairo asked in the background.

"Next to me. We checked out the tip with the mayor's niece."

"How did it turn out?" Aydin spoke.

I nibbled on my bottom lip. "I don't trust her."

"You don't trust anybody."

I smirked. "Then it's good that I'm biased with these cases."

"Biased or an asshole?" Aydin questioned.

"A little of both." I glared at Valencia when she hugged Yanira and stepped back inside the building.

"Get the car picked up, and we'll catch up with you," Aydin responded.

I removed the phone and looked at the time. "Should we tell Artemis?"

"If this was your sister, would you want to know?"

I stood off to the side and waited as Yanira approached me. "Fuck, you're right." I promised to keep Artemis included. Her family would want answers.

"Set up a meeting," Aydin said.

"Copy that." I ended the call as Rye finished his conversation.

"The boys are coming to pick up the car and drive us back," Rye informed me.

Yanira avoided my stare. Whatever she thought Valencia knew would come to light, but my anger wouldn't be pretty if it put her in danger.

Chapter 7

Yanira

I leaned my head against the bathtub as I soaked up the silence. The past few days had taken a toll on my mental health and exhausted me physically. My family was worried, and I wasn't sure things would work out in my favor with the lack of updates from the police. Campbell and Kristen seemed standoffish with me investigating my case, and I hated to put them in the middle, but I needed answers. Someone was out to get me, and I didn't know who to trust. Maybe going into this line of work was foolish, and I needed to focus on a less intense occupation. Even my brother wanted to protect me, which would take him away from his family. We were protective of each other and would fight any battle if it meant saving the other.

I sat up and drained the tub. "I'm turning into a prune."

After I dried off, I stepped out of the bathroom in a robe. I rubbed lotion on my hands and went to open my bag on the bed, removing a pair of panties and a bra. I picked up my phone to see that I had a few missed calls from Farrah. Throwing on a pair of shorts and an oversized shirt, I dialed her number.

She laughed at the other end of the call. "Yanira, hey. Remembered your best friend?" Farrah loved to get on my nerves.

I sighed, picked up my comb, and brushed my hair. "Sorry, Farrah."

"Why has it taken you so long to get in touch?"

I paused and glanced around the room. "Still at this prison."

She cackled. "With the sexy Navy man?"

Once finished with my hair, I lifted the phone, stood up to look at myself in the mirror, and rolled lip gloss on my lips. "Farrah, please. I don't see him like that."

"From what I've seen, he's sexy and tall," she replied.

I slipped my feet into my house shoes and headed out of the bedroom.

"We should have lunch tomorrow."

I walked down the hall into the kitchen. Bishop stood at the stove with a beer in his hand.

He had on shorts and no shirt and stood with his back to me. "Yanira?"

"Let me call you back." Not in the mood to hear Farrah's jokes with him here, I hung up.

Bishop turned to face me and tipped his chin. "Are you hungry?"

"I could eat." I sat on the stool.

He turned back to the skillet, flipped the food, and turned off the stove.

"What did you think yesterday?"

Bishop glanced over his shoulder. "About?"

"My source."

"Nothing to say. You need sources for the stories."

I crossed my legs. "So you don't think it was bad I used the employee of the mayor's office to get information?"

Bishop picked up the skillet and poured a small amount of pasta on one plate before he reached for another plate. "It's a bold move, but I can't say it was bad."

I took the fork out of his hand. "Do you think they'll find out who's stalking me?"

"Police are on the case, but I have some ideas."

"Oh?"

"In addition to you staying here, we put a few cameras around your place and bugged your office."

I covered my mouth after I slipped some food inside. "My office?"

He sat across from me and started to eat. "In my opinion, it's an inside job."

I sighed. "So much happening. I want my life back."

"You'll have it soon."

We made eye contact, and I giggled at the red sauce on the corner of his mouth.

"What's so funny?"

I shook my head and pointed my finger at the sauce. "You have a little something."

"On my face?"

I nodded and laughed as he tried to wipe it off and smeared it on his chin.

He narrowed his eyes. "You think it's funny?"

I doubled over and grabbed my stomach. "Sorry, it's on your chin now."

He picked up the napkin.

"Wait, let me do it." I snagged the napkin from his hand.

He stood in front of me and let me clean him off.

"There you go."

I held the napkin out to him, and he grasped my hand to take it back. Our eyes locked.

"You have something..." He pointed at my nose.

"No, I don't."

He dipped his fork in the sauce and dripped a little onto my nose.

"You're an asshole." I turned and grabbed another napkin, wiping my face as he chuckled. "How does your girlfriend put up with you?" I finished my food and laid my fork down.

Bishop picked up the plates and took them to the sink. "No girlfriend."

I strolled to the fridge and grabbed a beer. "So, you're just an asshole to me?"

He ignored my question. "Artemis know you drink?"

I faked a laugh and sauntered up to him. "I'm grown." I lifted the beer to my lips and took a sip. "Seems you're more worried about my brother than me."

Bishop took it out of my hands, drank the rest, and planted it on the counter. "No one scares me, Yanira."

"Sure about that?" I cocked a brow.

"Positive." He smirked.

I glanced from his eyes to his lips. Leaning into his chest, I stood on my toes and pressed a kiss to his lips. Bishop cupped my face and sucked my tongue into his mouth.

I grabbed his arms to keep myself upright. "Mmhmm..."

Bishop pulled away and winked at me, then slid a hand down my back. "Are you sure?" He ran a finger over my lips.

"Don't stop."

His steady gaze traveled over my face and searched my eyes. "You are so beautiful."

"Take me to bed."

He scooped me up and carried me out of the kitchen. It

was out of character for me to instigate sex with a man. Usually, they did the flirting, but Bishop was different. I helped remove his shirt, and he cupped my butt, stopping halfway and placing me down.

He pressed his long, hard shaft between my legs and pulled my shirt open. "We won't make it to the bedroom."

My legs went around his waist, and I licked my lips. "Take me right here, Bishop."

Bishop leaned down and kissed me from my breasts to my lips. He pushed his pants down and slid inside me with a slow stroke that left me speechless.

Bishop groaned. "Yanira, I knew you would be my weakness."

"Good thing you can handle the pressure."

Our hands connected, and he stretched my arms above my head, thrusting harder. My breath hitched, and I whimpered in delight as his large body covered mine.

"Oh," I groaned.

"Uh...Mmhmm." He pumped in and out.

"Bishop. Yes, Bishop."

He pulled back and watched me. "You know this isn't part of the bodyguard services."

The idea sent my spirits soaring. "You're fired."

"Fucking crazy, Yanira." He shook his head and moved his hands to my thighs. Kissing alongside my neck. Not ready for it to end, we stood entangled together and walked down to his room. I leaned up and sucked on his neck. "Hopefully, a good crazy."

Bishop kissed me softly and rubbed my thighs. His eyes drank me in as he slowly pushed forward. "Yanira! Shit." He moaned and brought me to the best orgasm of my life.

* * *

My head pounded, and I groaned as a phone rang. Keeping my eyes closed, I felt around for it, and my hand landed on something warm and hairy. My eyes popped open to see a sleeping Bishop. I peeked beneath the covers and realized I was naked.

"Bishop," I mumbled. I closed my eyes and rubbed my aching forehead as the phone continued to ring.

"Mmmmm," Bishop muttered under his breath, as he gripped me tighter.

I poked him in the arm. "Bishop."

"Yanira, I let you go on top," Bishop mumbled, turning to his back.

"Bishop, wake up!" I whined.

"What's wrong?"

I sat up and covered my chest with the covers. "Your phone is ringing."

He reached for his phone as I turned to grab my shorts.

"Where are you going?"

"Back to my room." I knew this wasn't a love or relationship situation, and I would never wait for a man to kick me out. Feelings weren't that deep that I'd cause a problem after what we did.

He shook his head. "Hello?"

I walked back to my bedroom to shower and get dressed.

Later that afternoon. Bishop, Rye, and I met with the mayor in his office. My skin crawled from simply being in the same room as him, after all the dodgy stunts he'd pulled —from paying off seats to get votes in the city council to putting his people on the police force. He'd snuck his way into being a slumlord by disguising it with fake shell companies.

Mayor Keller unbuttoned his jacket and sat down.

"Bishop, this is a surprise." Mayor Keller was the worst corruption I had ever seen.

"Not for me," I mumbled under my breath.

Mayor Keller's eyes narrowed on me. "Do I know you?"

"Mr. Mayor, please don't insult me," I growled.

"Yanira," Bishop warned.

I rolled my eyes and pushed my hair behind my ear. "What?"

Bishop might have thought I should be quiet, but the mayor knew the truth.

He rubbed his chin. "Yanira. That name sounds familiar." He snapped his fingers and smiled. "Ah, yes. The lady reporter."

"She's our client," Bishop informed him.

His eyebrows rose wide. "Client? Why?"

I couldn't hold my tongue any longer. "Please! Like you don't know what you've done."

Bishop placed his hand on my lower back.

Mayor Keller leaned back in his chair. "Why the hostility?" He smirked, clasped his hands together, and stared at me.

"Yanira believes the story she was working on has something to do with her editor being killed and her ending up with a stalker."

"What does that have to do with me?"

"Have you read the story?" I lifted the newspaper off the table near the couch, unfolded it, and laid it on his desk. I pointed at the article with my name up top.

The mayor *called into question over renters' rights.*

Keller read the title and his brows bunched together. "This must be a mistake. I don't have any renters."

"Sir, you can lie to the folks out there"—I gestured at the door—"but not to me."

He tossed the paper aside and glared at me. "Why are you in my office with these frivolous accusations?"

"Not frivolous, and I have sources." I smiled.

He waved off my comment. "Lies from a nobody, and you think that's going to, what? Take me down?" He scoffed.

"In due time."

"Do you have any dealings with the apartments named in the article?" Bishop asked.

"I hope you're not suggesting I had something to do with killing someone?" Keller's eyes narrowed.

"We need to cover everything in detail," Bishop said.

Mayor Keller held a staring match with Bishop. "My lawyer will have this story thrown out with an apology."

"I'll never apologize or retract a story," I stated.

He smirked. "Once the lawsuit I bring about that fake ass newspaper is out, you'll do more than apologize."

Bishop charged at him and gripped him around the neck, forcing his head down on the desk. "I may have worked for you before, but you've crossed the line. Apologize."

Rye tried to pry his hands off him. "Bishop, no."

Mayor Keller tried to remove Bishop's hands from his neck. "I'll have you arrested for assaulting a public figure!" Keller spluttered.

Bishop squeezed his neck harder.

Keller's secretary popped her head into his office. "Mr. Keller, I have your—what on earth is going on in here?"

He released Keller and fixed his jacket. Mayor Keller held his chest, then loosened his tie to catch his breath. "Call the police!" Keller demanded.

"I'm calling security," the secretary responded.

"We're leaving." I tried to get Bishop focused on me.

Bishop got in his face and didn't budge. "Apologize or else," Bishop growled.

"Sorry," Keller mumbled.

"Bishop, it's okay." I rubbed his arm.

Mayor Keller snarled at Bishop, and held eye contact, something deeper was at play between them.

"I came in here and saw him with his hands around the mayor's neck." The secretary returned with a security guard and pointed at Bishop.

The short, chubby guard looked Bishop up and down and reached for the mace in his pocket.

"We're leaving. No need to call for backup," Rye assured the guard.

I grabbed Bishop's hand and walked out of the office. "What was that back there?" I demanded as we headed for the elevator.

"Keller's a jerk, but he's also dangerous and underhanded," Bishop muttered.

The elevator dinged, and a group of people stepped off. I moved to the side as Bishop pushed for the lobby and scrubbed a hand on the back of his neck. I worried he could be arrested since Keller liked to pretend he's in charge.

Chapter 8

Bishop

Only thing I wanted was to hurt Keller for the way he came at Yanira. Even if she was wrong no one would disrespect her in my presence. The doors pinged as a few people moved around to leave.

"Hi, Yanira," a low voice spoke.

Yanira looked at the young man as he stepped out of the elevator. "Oh, hi, Jet."

I waited for Yanira and let the elevator doors close without us.

"What are you doing here?" she asked.

He held up a slip of paper and shrugged. "Jury duty."

"This late?" Yanira looked at her watch.

Jet glared for a second, and then a smile appeared. "Since this morning."

Yanira pushed the elevator button. "Oh, well. It's good to see you."

"Are you back at the office?" Jet asked.

"Unofficially, but I'm not letting anyone keep me from my job."

"True. You're the best reporter we have." Jet smiled.

"Yanira, I have a meeting. We need to head out," I said.

Yanira moved closer to me. "Yeah, right. Sorry, Jet. I'll see you around." She waved as the elevator doors closed.

Rye tucked his badge in his pocket. "Who's that?" Rye asked.

Yanira scratched her nose, then shoved her hands in her pockets. "He works at the newspaper with me." The smile she wore radiated through her even after the situation upstairs.

"How close are you two?"

She popped a piece of gum in her mouth. "What do you mean?"

"Does he know what's going on?" I clarified.

Yanira looked at me. "Everybody knows about me witnessing the murder."

The doors finally opened, and we headed out of the building. We trekked to the car and she climbed into the front seat. I walked around to the driver's side.

I stopped Rye before he could get in the car. "Do a check on Jet."

Rye pointed back at the building. "The kid we just saw?"

"He's not a kid. He's a grown man," I fussed, ignoring his comment.

Rye grinned and typed in his phone. "Is this jealousy or for the case?"

"You know me, Rye, not a jealous bone in my body. Could be nothing, but I'd rather check everyone out."

"Sure, no harm in that."

"Maybe Aydin already had a background check done, but after the situation at Valencia's, I want to triple-check."

"You like her?"

I sucked my teeth and pushed off the car. "What?"

"Do you like her?"

"I'm not entertaining this conversation."

"Shit. Cairo acted the same way with Bria." Rye chuckled.

As Rye went to the back passenger seat, I sensed someone staring. I looked up toward the building but didn't see anything. The strong feeling wouldn't escape me, but I shook it off. I hopped in and drove to Yanira's parents' house to drop her off and meet with the guys and run over a few questions.

* * *

Yanira promised she wouldn't leave and would wait until I came back to pick her up, so that gave me a few hours to talk with the team. The days and nights ran together, but our goal was always the same—to protect our client.

Cairo passed a folder to me. "How is she doing?"

"Fine for now. I was about to be arrested, but she calmed me down."

He stood in the entryway. "Arrested for what?" Soaquan quizzed.

"Almost choked the mayor."

Every mouth in the room dropped open.

He chuckled and marched in the room. "Are you sick?" Soaquan tried to touch my forehead.

"What?" I slapped his hand away, and they all laughed.

Soaquan grabbed the folder from me. "Must be love, then."

I glanced out of the blinds and saw Rye and Maddox at the front desk laughing as Rye's hands demonstrated something that looked like choking.

"Tell me exactly what happened because that's a big

leap from a conversation to almost choking the man," Aydin observed.

"He was disrespectful."

"Aydin knows all about being in love and how to protect his woman, so try not to end up in jail," Cairo joked.

"Cairo, you're in the same boat as Aydin and Maddux," Soaquan pointed out.

"How did I get pulled into this?" Maddux threw his hands up.

"All right, boys. Less time making Bishop blush and more time figuring out what Keller is up to, which might help solve the case," Aydin exclaimed.

"Rye and I took the information on Valencia and spoke with her."

"Did she give you anything?" Soaquan queried, passed the file back to me.

"Not much besides being the source for Yanira's story, but I think she's after something."

Sam sighed. "What could she possibly want?"

I flipped open the file and read through some of her background. "She's living pretty modestly, considering she's the mayor's niece."

"Her parents?" Cairo waited for me to respond.

"Died in a car crash."

Aydin rubbed his chin and leaned back in his chair. "Strange. The mayor doesn't seem like the loving type, and she wasn't seen with him during his campaigning."

Rye entered the room and said, "No, and usually they're the type to throw kids and family down our throats."

"Same thing I wondered about. I feel like she's up to something and not doing this out of kindness," I observed.

"Yanira say anything about her?" Soaquan asked.

"She seemed to be on her side," Rye responded.

I nodded. "Like she felt bad for her."

"Talk with Yanira a little more and see what you can find out. It may be the key to finding her stalker." Aydin gathered a stack of papers.

"Anything besides that?" Maddux asked.

I frowned. "Possibly nothing, but that Campbell guy might be sleeping with the new editor."

"You sound like the housewives show my wife watches." Maddux chuckled.

"I got this from Yanira, but it's something we should concentrate on."

"Any footage from the car incident the other day?" Cairo checked with Aydin, and a video screen popped up of the street where Valencia lived.

Aydin stood, walked over to the screen, and pointed at the cameras in the video. "They have a shot from the right corner. You can see a few people talking, and the building has a camera, but it was broken that day." He played the clip for us.

"Whoever did it knew to hide." I watched myself run out to the road.

"Take the footage to the cops and see what they say. Maybe Owen can give us some insight from the traffic lights," Aydin instructed.

"All right, and I'll let you know after I see what Campbell is up to," I replied.

"Aren't Campbell and Yanira rival reporters?" Aydin probed.

"Either way, I'll be as professional as I was with the mayor."

* * *

Laughter echoed through the walls of the police station. I headed down the hall to meet with Owen and see how far things had gotten with Yanira's case. I had a feeling they'd pushed her case to the side.

Maddux and Rye trailed alongside me as Owen rose from his seat to shake our hands.

Owen fixed his holster and sat down. "Gentlemen, I didn't know we had a meeting today."

"Last minute thing," I said. "I haven't heard from you and wanted to know if there were any updates on Yanira's case."

"I'm slammed with so much right now. I'm waiting on forensics on the knife used to kill the editor," Owen replied and gestured at a stack of folders on his desk.

My brow hiked up. "Yanira's case is a priority. That was clear when I was pushed to take on the role of her bodyguard."

Owen raised both hands in the air. "Listen, man, this is not my idea, but from the top."

"The top?"

"Yeah, I got told by the chief to focus on other things."

"Since when does the chief get that deep into your cases?" I demanded.

"It happened earlier today."

"What time?" Rye investigated.

"Shit. I don't remember. As soon as I got here this morning, I had a message to call him back," Owen answered.

Rye and I looked at each other. "The mayor," we said in unison.

"Fill me in because I'm lost." Maddux watched us.

"Me, too." Owen crossed his arms.

To hear that Owen's chief had pushed him to back off,

more than likely at the mayor's request, meant Yanira was on her own if anything happened to her.

Keller had overstepped his boundaries because of what I did to him at his office. The chief of police having Owen out of the loop would make things even more difficult. Luckily, Aydin had a relationship with a few people higher up in the political ring. I'd need to make some calls.

"Keller is the reason you've been taken off the case," I explained.

Owen pursed his lips. "Mayor Keller?"

"The one and only."

"Why?"

"To get back at me. I...may have tried to choke him."

Owen's eyes popped wide. "Choked the mayor? Are you crazy?"

"Aydin already yelled at me."

Owen rubbed his forehead and reached for his phone.

"Who are you calling?"

"The chief to see if it was the mayor," Owen answered, dialing the chief's number. "Chief, this is Owen. I'm sitting here with Bishop and some of the guys from the unit. Call me back." Owen left a voice message and hung up.

"Aydin sent us to look at some footage and maybe get screenshots from traffic cameras."

"What day?" Owen inquired.

I handed him the USB. "A few days ago, someone busted the window and shot out the tires in my car."

Owen stared at me. "Yanira is probably safer in police custody than with you."

I waved him off. "She's safe with me."

"I'll look at the footage and see what I can do, but now I'm off the case, it may take a while." Owen slipped on his glasses.

"I know I'm putting you in a bad position, but I need the information."

"Yanira must be important to you."

"More than you know."

Owen's phone rang, and he lifted a finger to indicate we should wait as we stood to leave. "Hey, Andy. I need your help with something. About to send over some footage now." Owen pulled the phone away from his ear. "I might not be able to look it over myself, but he didn't say someone else couldn't."

* * *

"Hell, no! I want that story. You know me, Richard. I don't play games." Campbell slammed the phone down and picked up his cigarette.

I flipped through my notes as he glared at me. "Campbell, the reporter known for doing anything it takes to get the story, even if it's false. Sometimes even paying for fake documents to make it look legit."

"Not true." He puffed on his cigarette.

"Isn't it against the law to smoke in an office?" Rye asked.

Campbell shrugged. "Not my problem, and what's so urgent you had to interrupt my afternoon meeting?"

"The one with Kristen?"

Campbell tapped his pen on the table. "My editor, yes."

"How is your relationship with Yanira?"

He gnawed on his bottom lip. "Fine." His arrogance would be his downfall.

"She has a different version."

"All women do." He grinned.

I narrowed my eyes. "Professional relationships can often be strained."

"If she weren't a bitch, I would say we could work together."

My fists balled up. "Her name is Yanira."

Campbell scoffed. "Is there a reason for this meeting? Otherwise, I need to be out of here to catch up on a story."

"How long have you and Kristen been sleeping together?"

"A few weeks."

"Usually, people deny sleeping with the boss."

"I'm not most people."

"To save us both some time, tell me if you've been stalking Yanira."

He cackled at my comment. "To stalk Yanira, I would have to care, and I don't. My career is far beyond hers. The work she does is garbage."

"Kristen cut Yanira off and put you on the biggest story, and you don't think it's because you're sleeping together?"

The door flew open, and Kristen appeared. She glared at Campbell. "What the hell is wrong with you?"

"Kristen! Calm down and wait for me in your office," Campbell ordered.

"No! Your wife called and threatened me," she snarled.

Campbell jumped up, walked around his desk, and grabbed Kristen's hand. She jerked back and slapped him across the face. She raised her hand again, but Rye grasped her wrist.

"Bitch!" Campbell charged at her.

I blocked him with my hand. "I need you both to calm down!"

Campbell tried to yank out of my hold. "Don't forget who made you!" he gritted through his teeth.

Kristen tried to squirm out of Rye's arms. "If you think for one second you can manipulate me, think again, asshole."

"Shut up, Kristen," Campbell hissed.

She chortled. "If I go down, you'll be right there with me."

"I said, shut up!"

"Fuck you, Campbell!"

"Kristen, what is it that Campbell has on you?" I asked.

Kristen suddenly seemed to realize she had an audience. Her shoulders slumped, and Rye released her. "Nothing. Sorry, I was just in my head about something."

Rye blocked her as she turned to leave. "No, we're all going to sit and have a conversation."

"Campbell?" Kristen called his name.

He rolled his eyes. "Now you want to listen to me?"

I glared at them. "What have you two done?"

Kristen wiped a tear and sat down on the office couch. "We've been sleeping together."

"For how long?"

"A few months."

I glared at Campbell, who'd said it was a few weeks. "Did the previous editor know about this affair?"

Kristen shook her head. "It was just between us two."

"Look, our relationship had nothing to do with the editor's murder or Yanira," Campbell announced.

The statement caused Kristen to jump up quickly. "You don't think I killed my boss?"

"Everybody is a suspect."

"But Campbell and I have nothing to do with our editor's murder that night because we—" She paused and bit her lip.

"You what?" I asked.

"Might as well tell them since you gave everything else away." Campbell went back to his desk.

"Oh, shut up, Campbell, and call your wife before I have her arrested."

I let out a frustrated sigh. "Can you two focus on me and leave the petty arguing to later?"

"Bitch," he mumbled.

"Campbell got us a hotel the night the editor was killed."

"All night?"

Kristen answered with a nod.

"What hotel?"

"No, you're not snooping into my business affairs," Campbell barked.

"The second your affair hindered Yanira, it became our business."

Kristen responded. "The hotel two blocks from here."

"The Quinton Hotel?"

"Yes." Kristen lowered her head in shame.

I reached into my pocket, grabbed a pen, and passed it to her. "Give me the room number, date, and time."

"Come on, guys, us men all have a little something on the side," Campbell pleaded.

I took the paper out of Kristen's hand and strolled out of his office with Rye following me.

"An affair, murder, and stalker. This shit is like an episode of *Murder, She Wrote*," Rye muttered.

I stopped and tilted my head. "*Murder, She Wrote*?"

"Yeah, Jessica Fletcher was on it with her cases. Grew up watching her show." Rye chuckled.

I pushed the elevator button and ignored the conversations around the office. Out of the corner of my eye, I saw Jet laughing with a woman at her office door.

"Are you going to tell Yanira about Campbell?" Rye got on the elevator and hit the lobby button.

"She needs to know what she's up against." The doors closed as Jet passed by.

Kristen, Campbell, and Mayor Keller had reasons to set up Yanira. Maybe all three were working together and trying to take out Yanira to throw me off.

Rye slid the key in the ignition and drove me back to my place while I waited for Yanira to call.

Chapter 9

Bishop

A week later

My hand found her scalp, and I rubbed my fingers through her hair. I placed a soft kiss on her forehead, her temple, and her nose. Slipping my finger between her legs, I teased her swollen nub until she was panting. Yanira begged me to fuck her while I teased her, and I loved her cries of passion.

She whimpered as I held her legs wide and lapped at her sweet wetness. "Oh, yes, Bishop." Her body entranced me.

"You missed me."

All she could do was nod.

"Turn over, baby."

Quickly, she got on all fours and arched her back. I moved behind her and spread her legs wider. She shivered under my touch, and pre-cum leaked from my cock.

"You make me crazy, Yanira." I entered her with one swift thrust, sinking deep into her pussy.

"Fuck!" she screamed and dropped her head to the covers.

"Ah, shit, Yanira," I grunted.

I buried my face in her hair as my orgasm slammed through me.

* * *

I dragged a hand down my face. Rye and I were sitting outside Valencia's apartment. After the talk with Owen, I figured we should see if Keller made contact with his niece.

"This is a surprise," Rye muttered.

I looked up from my phone to see two black SUVs parked alongside her building. Keller stepped out of one with his assistant.

"Anytime we were on his detail, he never came here."

"Makes you wonder why now." Rye picked up the binoculars and watched Keller yell at his assistant and march up to Valencia's building.

"We need to get inside and hear what they're talking about."

"His niece might not like that."

"Neighbor, probably." Rye pointed at an old lady with a dog entering the building. We jumped out of the car and jogged across the street before the door closed. One of Keller's men stood at the door while Keller knocked and waited. We stood off in the corner to avoid being seen.

"Why are you here?" Valencia snapped.

"My favorite person in the world," Keller replied.

Valencia tapped her foot on the floor. "I told you not to come here anymore."

"Valencia, I'm your uncle. Can I come inside and talk?" Mayor Keller tried to be calm.

"No," she hissed.

"Valencia, either you let me in, or your little trust fund will be no more," Keller spat.

Valencia shoved him back and pointed in his face. "You disgust me."

"Not the first time I've heard that."

Valencia wiped a tear from her cheek. "My parents must be turning in their graves."

Mayor Keller gripped her wrist and shoved her backwards. "Your parents should have taught you to respect your elders."

I ended the back and forth, swiftly approaching as Valencia tried to hit her uncle and was blocked by his security.

"Mayor Keller, do we have a problem here?" I watched Keller and Valencia's eyes widen in surprise.

Mayor Keller dragged his gaze from me to Valencia. "This is a private matter between my niece and me."

"Doesn't seem like she wants you here." I pointed to her balled-up fists.

Valencia unclenched them and stood straight. "As my uncle said, it's private."

"Anything you want to tell me, Valencia?"

Valencia glared at her uncle. "No." Her dog barked behind her.

"See? She's just a little upset. I can handle it from here." Keller fixed his jacket.

"How much of her trust fund do you control?" I blurted.

Valencia gasped in shock, propping her hands on her hip.

"None of my private family business is of your concern. I believe our last conversation ended with you no longer working for me," Keller grumbled.

"Valencia?"

"My uncle and I are fine," she replied, quickly shutting the door. The person she called an uncle only wanted what was best for him and she still tried to save him.

Keller glared at me and stomped out of the lobby.

"She's hiding something, but we need to give her space," Rye reminded me.

I blew out a breath. "Great. Another potential suspect." My phone vibrated with a text.

Yanira: *Hey, are you busy?*

As I lifted my phone and opened the car door, I saw the same elderly lady come out of the building.

Me: *I'm on my way to you.*

I pushed the phone back into my pocket and sprinted toward the woman. "Excuse me, ma'am."

"Yes?"

"Sorry to bother you, but my sister lives a few doors down from you. Brunette, and about your height."

"Oh, yes. Valencia. Poor thing has been through so much." She lifted the trash bin and tossed her garbage inside.

"Have you seen many people come and go to her place? Our uncle was just here."

She glanced left to right and leaned in to whisper, "That man is a disgrace, but Valencia isn't so innocent either."

"What do you mean?"

"A few times, I've heard her yelling back and forth with him, and then they were kissing," she muttered in disgust.

The building door opened, and a few people walked out laughing.

"I've said too much." She shook her head and rushed back inside.

"What was that about?" Rye inquired.

I sighed, rubbing my forehead in confusion. "More questions than answers. I don't think Valencia is who she says she is."

"What do you mean?"

"I need to talk to Yanira."

Rye started the car, and I opened my message thread as he drove.

Yanira: *Back in the saddle, and Kristen is letting me pitch a new story.*

Me: *That's great.*

Yanira: *How about dinner tonight? My treat to celebrate?*

Me: *Works for me, but it's my treat.*

Yanira: *You're not paying.*

Me: *Habit, but I'll talk to you soon. I have another call.*

I've never had a woman in my life besides a few dates here and there, and I didn't know how to consider another person. Yanira was still at my place, and we'd gotten closer, but she wanted to go out to get a sense of normalcy. I had been against it because we hadn't caught the person stalking her, and I didn't want to give either of us the wrong impression. Women never stayed in my life for long, and I now had someone who relied on me. It made me realize what I'd missed by not being more open in the past.

Chapter 10

Yanira

"**S**omething tells me you've met someone." Naarah walked around the couch and sat next to me. She giggled and bumped my shoulder.

I played with my nephew as he pushed his favorite train set around the room. "Can't I just be happy?"

Her features became more animated. "Happy from what?"

"Living a healthy life."

She laughed. "Artemis told me about the guy you're staying with."

A warm glow flowed through me when I thought about Bishop. "He's my bodyguard, assigned to protect me."

She poked me in the side. "Protecting not only your body but also your heart. I see that smile."

"How are things with you and my brother?"

"Good. We had a lot of fun on our trip."

I turned to see her make googly eyes and gasped in shock. "You're pregnant!"

Naarah held a finger to her lips. "Shush."

"Mommy's pregnant." Artemis Jr. clapped his hands.

"Do you know what that means, nephew?" The best thing in life is being an aunt to a beautiful bright baby boy. AJ surprised us every day with the way he learned things so fast.

He swung his head from left to right.

"It means you'll be a big brother." I held a hand up to him for a high five.

Naarah waved me off. "I wanted to wait before I told everybody." She leaned back on the couch and pulled her feet up underneath her.

I reached over and hugged her. "My brother knows, right?"

"No. I took the test yesterday and haven't had a chance to tell him." Naarah knew her husband would probably have her on bedrest from the moment he found out she was pregnant.

"We'll keep our mouths shut so you can surprise him."

Artemis Jr. and I pretended to zip our mouths closed.

Naarah propped her head on her hand as she sat facing me on the couch. "Tell me about this suspension at work."

"Well, technically, it's not a suspension. I'm working from home."

Naarah scratched her cheek. "Artemis said there's a stalker."

"I walked in on my boss *dead* in his office," I whispered to avoid my nephew from hearing me.

"That's terrible! Are you all right?"

I clasped my hands together. "Now I am, but it's been scary. To think someone hates me that much."

"Any leads?"

"No, and I'm worried this will go on forever."

"Have the police gotten any closer to finding the person?"

"None, and it's crazy because I think the mayor is behind everything."

She looked shocked by my admission. "The mayor?"

I nodded. "Before my boss died, I worked on a story involving him."

My mom stepped into the living room with a towel in her hand. "Dinner's ready." She bent to pick up my four-year-old nephew.

"Grandma, we're pregnant!"

"What are you talking about, little boy?" She tickled him on his stomach.

"Just like his auntie. Messed up the surprise." Naarah stood and took him from Mom, kissing his cheek.

"Y'all better tell me what he's talking about."

"What did you cook for dinner?" I asked to distract her.

"Chili and rice." She swatted me on the butt. My dad and brother sat at the table and wrapped up their card game as Naarah sat next to Artemis.

Mom cleared the table and went into the kitchen to grab the food. She placed the bowl on the table.

"Smells good." I picked up a bowl and spooned a small amount for my nephew.

Naarah cut a piece of cornbread for him. "There's something I wanted to talk to everyone about."

"How is everything in your case? I haven't talked to Bishop to get an update?" Artemis asked.

"Naarah first." I scooped up some chili and cornbread together.

Naarah placed a hand on top of my brother's and smiled. "I'm pregnant."

Both my mom and dad smiled and rose to kiss Naarah and my brother.

"You serious, baby?" Artemis planted a hand on her stomach and kissed her on the lips.

My nephew tried to extend his arm around my brother and hug them both. "Mommy is having a baby."

"You'll be a big brother." Artemis picked up his son and kissed him on the forehead.

"Yay!" He laughed.

"We have to plan a baby shower and christening," Mom said excitedly.

I cackled. "Ma, she's not even showing."

"Well, we have to start early. I'll probably be seventy by the time you have a baby," she joked.

"Serious talk, Yanira. How is everything with Bishop?" Artemis wondered.

"Good. We get along fine." I blew over the chili to cool it off.

Naarah helped my nephew wipe his hands.

My phone buzzed, and I placed my spoon down to grab it from my pocket.

Bishop: *When you're ready, call me for a ride.*

Me: *I can have my brother drop me off.*

Bishop: *Don't argue with me.*

I smiled.

Mom jested. "See that smile on her face?"

Me: *Yes, sir. I'll be ready in an hour.*

Bishop: *Good. Tell everyone I said hello.*

"Bishop says hello, and he's close to figuring out who's stalking me."

"Maybe you should change jobs," Dad announced as he popped open another beer.

"Daddy, please. You know I love my job." Sometimes they wanted to put me back in my childhood room and act like I never grew up.

Dad responded, "Not safe, Yanira."

"I want to meet this Bishop for real with a sit down and meal after all this stalker business is finished." My mom slipped another bowl of chili on the table.

"You will one day."

Mom muttered, rolling her eyes, "Hopefully, before the next baby comes."

"Not funny. Anyway, I'll be back at work soon, and no one will keep me from doing what I love."

"A stalker is not a little thing, Yanira," Artemis remarked.

"I know that, Artemis, but you act like I wanted this to happen."

"Yanira!" Mom scolded.

"It's true. Dad and Artemis want me to be some scared little bird, and that's not me." I threw my napkin on the table and paced in the living room.

"All my life, I had to protect you." Artemis stood near the couch and stared at me.

I stuck my tongue out at him. "That's the point of a big brother."

"Your protector."

"Yes, an annoying brother who spoils his little sister." I poked my lip out.

He chuckled and reached his arms out for me to hug him.

"I missed you when I was on active duty and didn't get a chance to be overprotective, so I try to make up for that."

My head fell on his chest. "Believe me, you've done a good job."

Artemis squeezed me close, kissed the top of my head. "Whoever is after you will get caught and wish they never met the family behind you."

"I know, bro." I patted him on the chest, stared at the open layout at the table of people I called family, and felt myself become more vulnerable.

Artemis plucked my nose. "Then don't shut me out. I worry more if I don't know what's going on with you."

"You have a family of your own."

"Doesn't matter. You'll always be my first baby."

We smiled and hugged each other, then pulled apart at the knock on the door.

I lifted my wrist to check the time on my watch. "Who's that at this hour?"

"Bishop," Artemis said as he opened the door.

"Artemis, good to see you again." Bishop extended a hand, and Artemis shook it.

I cocked my head to the side. "Has it been an hour?"

"I figured I'd come early." Bishop stepped inside my parents' home.

"Are you hungry?"

Bishop responded, "I'm fine."

Artemis motioned for Bishop to follow him. "Maybe I can get some answers since my

sister's been quiet about the stalker case."

"Where are you going?" I asked.

Artemis gestured to the basement. "To talk. And you stay up here."

I felt like a little kid again, being left out of all the fun.

"Did I hear somebody at the door?" Naarah asked.

I nodded. "Yeah, Bishop."

"Bishop, your boyfriend?"

"My bodyguard."

Naarah stretched her arm around my shoulder and giggled. "Boyfriend who's a bodyguard."

"Turning into Mom, Naarah," I groaned and walked away from her.

* * *

Farrah ended her phone call and placed it on the table, and Chanel walked in, laughing on her phone. It seemed like everybody was in love lately.

"That big smile on your face must mean you'll be here for a few days," I said.

Chanel put her purse on the table. "Possibly. It depends on Maddux."

"How is Maddux doing?" Yanira inquired.

"Fine. Making me happy and driving me crazy at the same time," Chanel answered dramatically.

All of us burst into laughter.

"Married life." Farrah giggled.

"Farrah, I love your hair." Chanel picked up the menu.

"Thanks. I wanted a different style and told her to shave it off and color it blond."

"She's the only one who can pull it off," I responded, slipping a hand over her cut.

Farrah sipped on her water. "Not true, with your facial features and bone structure."

"I'm fine with my simple style." I flicked a hand through my curls.

"Fill me in on what I've missed," Chanel said.

Farrah quipped, "I'm in the same boat. Yanira's been on lockdown."

"Lockdown? Really, Farrah?" I smacked my lips.

Chanel ordered while our drinks were placed on the table. Lunch dates were few and far with us all spread out.

"Maddux told me about Bishop." Chanel checked her makeup in her compact mirror.

"He talks too much," I grumbled, avoiding eye contact.

"Men gossip as much as women." Farrah sipped on her drink.

"Bishop is fine. Surprisingly, we get along," I said.

Chanel pursed her lips. "I heard you're doing very well."

Farrah took her plate from the waitress and laid it on the table.

"And the job, any news on when you'll be back full time?" Farrah queried.

I gulped on my drink before answering. "The current editor is letting me work part-time from home."

Chanel and Farrah passed food back and forth.

"That's bullshit if you ask me," Farrah cursed.

"I know, but they claim it's a liability to have me at the office."

"How about you should have kept your mouth shut!"

At the loud exclamation, I turned in my seat to see Campbell and Kristin at a table together.

Farrah rose from the chair and I motioned to sit back down. "What are you looking at?" Farrah asked.

I placed a finger to my lips to be quiet. "That's my boss at the table with Campbell."

"Campbell? The jerk who tries to steal your stories?" Farrah asked.

"My question is, why are they out together?" I held up some napkins, then dropped them on the floor. I turned and picked them up to watch the back and forth.

"Keep your voice down, Campbell," Kristen hissed.

"Stay out of whatever they have going on," Chanel implored.

I straightened in my chair, answering, "You know me. I never stay out of anything when it comes to a story." I stood and sauntered over to the table.

"If he gets—" Campbell stopped as his eyes grew wide in surprise.

"Kristen. Campbell. Interesting to see you two here together."

"Leave," Campbell gritted.

"Hi, Yanira," Kristen mumbled and tried to sink lower in the booth.

My hand motioned between them. "Are you together?"

"That's none of your business," Campbell chided, sitting up straight.

"Campbell, lower your voice," Kristen murmured.

"Your conflict of interest is apparent right now."

"Yanira, please realize the better journalist gets the better stories, no matter who I'm sleeping with, which I won't confirm or deny."

"I wonder if the board would be okay with the editor and a reporter sleeping together."

"You fucking bitch!" Campbell jumped up and got in my face.

"Hey!"

I whirled at the familiar voice. Campbell backed up, and Kristen jumped out of her seat.

Bishop blocked my view and pointed at Campbell's face. "If you want to continue breathing, I suggest you think twice before talking to her again."

I grasped his arm. "Bishop."

"She's the one who jumped in our business." Campbell flicked me off.

Bishop grabbed his arm and twisted it behind his back.

"All right!" Campbell yelled in pain.

"Bishop, it's fine. We do this a lot at work," I pleaded, trying to calm him.

Bishop glared at Campbell. "Watch how you talk to her."

Campbell cleared his throat. "Sorry. For sure, man," Campbell said, more afraid of Bishop than losing his job.

"We were just leaving." Kristen picked up her keys, jacket, and purse.

My eyes stayed on her and Campbell. "I'll see you at the office, Kristen."

Kristen blew out a breath. "I'm not sure that's a good idea."

I kept my expression neutral. "I believe we can work out a deal."

Bishop released Campbell, took my hand, and escorted me back to our table.

"Did that just happen?" Farrah gestured to Campbell and Kristen in the corner, arguing. Campbell stormed off and left the restaurant.

"Sorry, I messed up our lunch date. I had a feeling something was going on between those two."

Chanel cocked her brow at Bishop. "Aren't you a sight to see here today. Going to tell your friend Maddux about you almost fighting over my girl's honor," Chanel teased.

"It's been a crazy day. Bishop is not fighting for my honor and leave Maddux from the conversation. I forgot they worked together. Bishop you know Chanel, this is my other friend, Farrah."

"Nice to meet you, Farrah." Bishop placed a hand on my lower back and squeezed.

"You too, Bishop. Hopefully, our girl isn't causing you too much trouble," Farrah teased. Bishop smirked and kissed my forehead. It was the first time he'd shown affection outside of his home.

"Ignore her, Bishop. Ladies, we'll get together again. Love you." I reached out to hug Farrah and Chanel before reaching into my wallet to leave some money.

Bishop pushed my hand away. "What are you doing?" he asked.

"About to pay."

He shook his head. "I already took care of the entire meal." Bishop grabbed my hand, and we all looked at him in astonishment.

"He's a keeper, Yanira," Chanel joked.

I chuckled. "Bye, y'all."

Bishop opened the restaurant door, and I stepped outside. The wind was chilly, and I rubbed my arms.

"You okay?"

I wrapped his arm around my waist to get warm. "I will be once Kristen lets me back on staff."

"We'll need to have someone with you all the time."

"I expected that."

"Good. Let's go home." Bishop pressed a kiss on my lips, took the keys out of my hand, and opened the car door for me to climb in.

Chapter Eleven

Jet

Once I saw Campbell storm out of the restaurant and Yanira left with Bishop, I knew Bishop must have confronted them. Kristen's dumb to think Campbell would be exclusive, and everyone at the office knew he was using her. I figured he'd dump her and move on, but to my surprise, they were still acting like a couple.

Bishop had to interrupt my fun and ruin the day I had planned for Yanira and me. She looked beautiful during regular hours at the office and extremely sexy outside of work.

I jumped at the knock on my car window and rolled it down. "Hi, Officer. Is there something wrong?"

"Your taillight is out."

"Oh, really?"

As he stood with one hand on his waist, he bent down and stared through the window. "Either you get that fixed today or get a ticket," he warned.

I tapped my fingers on the steering wheel, glancing in the rearview mirror. "Of course, sir. I had no clue."

"You young kids never do."

"Yes, sir."

"This parking spot is limited to an hour." He pointed at the sign. "I suggest you get moving."

I kept my mouth shut and turned the key. I threw my hand up that I would leave, and he stepped back as I pulled off. I looked over my shoulder as the police officer walked back to his car, and I slammed my hand on the steering wheel.

I did a U-turn, waiting for Bishop and Yanira to drive by. Five minutes later, her car drove past. I pushed the gas and tucked in behind them.

The day Yanira saw me at the courthouse, I wasn't truthful about my jury duty. I'd been watching her that day, and I'd had a meeting with my mentor, Mayor Keller. We'd formed a bond a few years back when he came to speak at my college campus, and he took me under his wing. He got me a job at the newspaper, and I was grateful forever.

I let two cars get in front of me, so I didn't look suspicious following Bishop back to his house. When Yanira went to her family's home for dinner the other night, I wanted to snatch her up then and bring her back to my basement. The security detail they put her under forced me to take more risks in public. I thought I had her the night I killed the editor, but she escaped and put a bigger target on my back.

Bishop approached his home and parked. I drove to the next block and turned around to keep a fair distance. If Yanira returned to the office, I'd have a clear view of her and could take her at any time. While she was at Bishop's, I had to jump through too many hoops to get her away from him. The night they became intimate, I wanted to run in and kill them both but restrained myself. Yanira only had so much time left before I made my move and took her from under his nose.

I reached into my pocket when my phone rang and smiled as I saw the caller. "Nice to hear from you."

"You get my message?"

"I did."

"Well, are you going to help me?"

I picked up my notepad and checked the time to jot it down. "I will talk to him."

"Great. I need this, Jet. You're the only one who can help."

"He's never going to marry you, Valencia."

A loud hiss creeped over the phone. "He will once I get pregnant."

I shifted in my seat. "Trapping the mayor won't make him fall in love with you." The woman was beyond delusional and hated to listen.

"Advice on love is the last thing I need from you."

I squinted, looking out the window, and watched traffic move in and out. "Keller isn't like your other sugar daddies."

"All I need is for you to talk to him."

"Aren't you tired of pretending to be a disgruntled tenant?"

"How do you know that?"

I removed the phone from my mouth and cursed under my breath. I'd staked out her apartment when Yanira and Bishop visited and overheard the conversation. "I have my ways."

"Something tells me your ways aren't legal."

"Try not to get us both kicked out of the will."

She snapped. "Fuck you, Jet."

I scoffed and ended the call, dropping my phone on the seat.

Valencia made appearances at Keller's campaign events for many years, and I thought it weird how he had her pretend to be his niece when she was his lover. Over time, I found out Yanira planned on writing a story about the issues with the buildings that Keller owned, and Valencia became the key source.

I checked my watch and saw it was almost 5 p.m. I reclined my seat and relaxed, picking up the sandwich I'd packed for dinner. A car was parked outside Bishop's home to keep watch, but they wouldn't see me.

* * *

I walked down the office halls and slid mail to the first two doors on the main floor for staff.

"Jet, did you get a package for me from fashion times?" the short blonde who handled style and culture for the newspaper asked.

"Not today, Sarah. Sorry."

She dropped her hands in her lap and blew out a breath. "Thanks. I told them I needed the pictures before noon."

"I'll keep an eye out for you."

She sat back in her chair, and I pushed the cart down the hall. When the elevator opened, a familiar voice reached me.

"If you don't upgrade my office, you'll wish I went with Detroit News!" Campbell barked on the phone.

I removed more mail and passed it over at the next stop. As I came out of the office, Campbell bumped into the cart.

"Watch it!" he yelled, then stomped into his office and slammed the door.

"Sorry, Mr. Campbell."

"Jet, come into my office, please," Kristen commanded.

I slid my phone back into my pocket and ignored Valencia's call.

"Shut the door." Kristen pointed behind me.

I shut the door behind me. "Is something wrong?"

Kristen plopped down in her seat, dropped her head for a brief moment. "I need a favor."

"A favor?" Kristen and I were never close.

"Mayor Keller is your friend and mentor, correct?"

"What do you need?"

Kristen folded her arms. "An interview."

"Not sure he'll go for that, Kristen."

Kristen stood with a frown, sauntered to me, and placed her hand on my shoulder. "Being in the mailroom isn't your life dream, is it?"

I glanced at her hand before stepping back. "I like my job."

She sighed. "An interview with Mayor Keller would help explain a lot of issues he's being accused of in the media."

"His business, not mine."

The door opened, and Kristen's assistant interrupted. "Sorry, Kristen. Yanira is at security downstairs and wanted confirmation she could come up," Madison said.

"I told her to wait for me to confirm with the board." Kristen whipped around to her desk and picked up the phone.

I walked out of her office as Campbell stormed past me. I stood in the corner of the hallway and watched them argue back and forth. A few minutes later, the elevator doors opened, and Yanira stepped out. A few coworkers approached her, and they hugged. She dropped the file box in her hand on the top of the desk, and Campbell marched over to her with Kristen following. I heard a little of their conversation.

"Yanira, welcome back," Campbell gritted through his teeth.

"Thank you, Campbell. I didn't expect you to be so nice." Yanira smirked.

"Look—"

Kristen interrupted before they could argue. "Campbell, you have a deadline. Please allow Yanira and me a few minutes to talk." She gestured for Yanira to come to her office.

Chapter 12

Yanira

Ten minutes before I parked my car and headed toward the employee entrance. I waved at the security guard at the door and hopped on the elevator toward my office floor.

I promised not to leave Bishop's house to work on my story, but after what I'd learned from Kristen and Campbell at the restaurant, I decided to make my comeback. It was still early, and most of the staff would be in the building, so I didn't think Bishop would be too mad.

Chanel: *Where are you?*

Me: *Sorry, I am running late. I had to stop at the office.*

Chanel: *I thought you took a leave of absence?*

The elevator doors opened. I started to text Chanel but decided to wait.

I dropped my phone on top of my box. "I came to bring some of my stuff back to the office."

"I thought you were on leave." Campbell walked alongside Kristen and me to my door.

I unlocked it and went inside. "Technically, I am but work never stops." I placed the box on the chair.

Kristen waited while I glanced around my office.

Campbell leaned on the doorframe. "You know they're trying to find the source of your story."

I closed the drawer and wiped a hand across the dust on my computer. "What story?"

"About what happened the night you ran out of the building."

"I told them I didn't want to be a story in the paper," I groaned, checking the stack of messages on my desk.

"Well, in this business, everybody is a potential story." Campbell left, and I shook my head in annoyance.

Most of the messages were work related, so I tossed them in the trash. "He's going to be your downfall."

"Campbell and I aren't together, but I need to clarify some things, Yanira."

I gestured to the chair. "Please have a seat."

"This won't take long." She continued to stand.

"Shoot."

"I plan on meeting with Mayor Keller to confirm the details of your story."

"Why?"

"Because you accused him of being a horrible landlord, and if it's not true, we'll be the subject of a lawsuit."

As I cocked my head to the side, I tapped on my computer. "How many sources do you have?"

Kristen tossed her hand in the air. "That's none of your business. I run this paper now, and you'll do as I say."

I gulped down the dryness in my throat. "His niece."

"What?"

"I confirmed the details from his niece."

Kristen perked up, pacing the floor. "Keller's niece?"

"Yes."

"I need her information." Kristen snapped her fingers and closed her eyes.

I wrote Valencia's number on a piece of paper. "She won't talk to you."

"Then you better make it happen because I'm not going down for this alone." Kristen stormed out of my office.

* * *

"Chanel, I'm sorry. I got carried away with work." I turned off the light in my office. It was past nine, and the staff had left hours ago. Chanel called to curse me out because I never responded to her texts from earlier.

"You left me hanging," Chanel accused.

After I grabbed my purse, I shut the door behind me and switched the phone to my left ear. "How can I make it up to you?"

Chanel pouted. "You can't."

"Don't be a brat." I laughed.

Chanel giggled. "Shut up. Maddux calls me a brat."

"Husbands know best." I pushed the button for the elevator and waited.

"Is Bishop picking you up?"

I glanced around the hallway and pulled my coat tighter to keep warm. "No, I drove." I tapped the elevator again.

"I thought he was supposed to be there at all times."

"He has men outside of the building waiting."

"Be careful, Yanira."

"I am."

"Farrah wants to organize a girl's trip soon."

I groaned. "Ugh."

"What's wrong?"

"This elevator is broken again." Plenty of people had complained, but the company never took it seriously, unless someone really hurt themselves.

"Can you call security?"

I walked down the hall. The entire floor was silent, only the air conditioner made noise. "Probably, but that'll take too long. I'll take the stairs."

"Maybe get security to escort you, Yanira."

"I'll just be a minute."

"Just feels weird."

I chuckled and reached in my pocket for my keys. "You worry too much." I shoved open the door for the stairs. A hand slipped over my mouth, and I dropped the phone. Before I could fight, something hit me over the head.

The last thing I heard was Chanel asking about the trip idea.

* * *

I woke up to pitch blackness and a massive headache. I should have listened to Chanel and called security before I left my office. Being stubborn had put me in a dangerous situation.

I tried to sit up but felt woozy. I rubbed my forehead. "What the hell?" Sticky blood clung to my fingers.

I slowly pulled myself up, my body sore. "Help!" I screamed.

A light came on, and my eyes fell on a dead body next to me. "Valencia?"

"She can't hear you."

I whipped my head up at the voice. No one was in the room, and it seemed like they were trying to disguise their voice.

I squinted my eyes, wiping them to see clearly. "Who are you?"

"All you had to do was stay away that night."

"Stay away?" I wished Bishop was with me and bossing me around because I would have never been in this situation if I listened to him.

They sighed. "I had no choice."

"You have a choice now. I can help you."

"I'm not dumb, Yanira."

"So you know my name."

He chuckled. "I know everything about you, Yanira. Artemis, your parents, and Farrah."

I gasped in shock. "Leave my family out of this!"

"Should have stayed away."

I scanned the room for anything I could use as a weapon. "You killed Everett."

"He caused his own death."

"Someone is going to know I'm missing." I prayed Chanel was able to get help.

"By that time, you'll be dead."

"Then face me! Show me your face." I knew Kristen saw me at the office, maybe she could get some help.

"Valencia got on my nerves," he said, voice dangerously low. Whatever she did must have really been bad for her to end up in this situation.

My eyes flew to Valencia's lifeless body. "Valencia's related to the mayor. You won't get away."

"The mayor will believe it was an accident."

"Where am I?"

He ignored my question. "Too many people will think you ran away."

"My family won't buy that crap."

"Campbell's right about you. You never shut up."

All the lights went out, and videos of me at different places played on the walls.

Chapter 13

Bishop

Rye and I stopped at the burger joint a block from the office and waited for Aydin and the boys to show up. Yanira decided to have dinner with Chanel, so I wasn't worried since we put someone on her surveillance.

Rye shoved the last of his burger in his mouth and gulped his beer. "What do we have so far?"

I wiped my hands and spread out the photos of each person we'd encountered who had issues with Yanira. Owen dropped off the video, which was still blurry, so we had no way to identify the vehicle.

"Kristen, Campbell, and Keller all had problems with Yanira," Rye remarked.

"His niece, who isn't really his niece, gave a story to Yanira."

"A story the niece used to get money."

The door swung open, and I heard the guys before I looked up. We all shook hands, and they took a seat.

"Columbo got some news," Aydin said.

"Tell me."

"Do you know Jet?"

"No. Should I?"

Rye rubbed his chin. "That name sounds familiar." He snapped his fingers. "He works at the newspaper with Yanira. The kid from the elevator."

Aydin's expression was serious. "We finally got a background check on everyone, and he jumped out."

"Why?"

Aydin pulled out some papers and dropped them on the table. "He's had Keller bail him out of a lot of problems. I think he killed Everett that night, and Yanira witnessed it. Everett probably discovered Jet's background, which was supposed to have been wiped clean."

"Yanira's at dinner right now." I jumped out of my seat.

Soaquan grasped my arm. "We do this the right way and call the police in case Keller tries to get involved." He picked up his phone and sent a text message.

Everyone sprinted out to the cars.

Rye jumped in the driver's seat. "How dangerous is he?"

"A few robberies and assault charges," Aydin answered.

"It was a cover-up from the beginning." I glanced at Aydin.

Soaquan talked on the phone. "Keller needs to know."

"If we tip him off, it'll only put Yanira in danger. Wait to call him." I reached into my pocket to call Yanira. "She's supposed to be at dinner with Chanel."

No answer.

Rye swerved in and out of traffic. "Call Chanel."

Chanel mumbled, "Hey, Bishop."

I turned down the radio and motioned for everybody to be quiet. "Chanel, are you with Yanira?"

"No, she never showed up for dinner."

"Are you sure?"

"Yeah, I spoke to her earlier. She was at the office."

"Fuck!" I barked.

Chanel panicked. "Is something wrong?"

I heard rustling on the other end and Maddux's voice.

"She's not answering her phone, and I thought she'd be with you by now."

Chanel whimpered, voice low. "If something is wrong, Bishop, you need to tell me."

"We know who's been stalking her."

"Who?"

I opened and closed my fist, pissed I missed the signs. "Jet."

"Jet?"

"A coworker."

A quietness filled the air between us. "Oh, my God. I need to find her," Chanel rambled.

"No, stay with Maddux. I have Aydin, Soaquan, Rye, and the police headed there now."

"Please call me as soon as you know something," Chanel pleaded.

I'd never wanted to get close to someone and have them in danger. I knew I would go to the deep end to save them.

"I will." I hung up with Chanel.

"Aydin still behind us?" I looked over my shoulder through the back window.

Rye ran through the red light and hopped on the freeway. "Yeah, and I know what you're thinking. We'll get her back safe."

"We better."

* * *

Ten minutes later, we arrived at the office building. Rye slammed on the brakes, and we jumped out when security came out of the building.

"Where's Teddy!" I shouted, scanning the parking structure for lead guard we assigned for her building.

"I don't see them." Rye followed me to the door.

Soaquan sprinted over to us.

"Can I help you, gentlemen?" the security guard questioned.

"Has anyone come and gone in the last hour?" I asked.

He crossed his arms over his chest. "What's this about?"

"We don't have time for conversation. Has Yanira come out of this building alone?" I pointed at the doors.

"No, it's just cleaning staff." He plopped his hands on his belt.

"Fuck! Soaquan, get some people to my house. Rye, follow me to her office."

"Bishop, we'll get her back," Aydin said as police officers arrived.

"Did someone call the police?"

"I don't have time to explain. We need the entire building on lockdown." I made for the elevator before deciding it would take too long and headed for the stairs.

Rye was right behind me, and we both removed our guns as we reached Yanira's floor.

"Cairo texted. She's not at your house," Rye whispered.

"Where else would he take her?"

"His place."

I thought that was too easy. "Put some people on his place, but I doubt he'd do something that simple."

Rye and I marched through the office.

"What about Keller's place?"

I froze at the mention of Keller and lowered my gun.

"Keller and Valencia," we said in unison.

I ran to Yanira's office and kicked open the door. Everything appeared to be in place.

"Bishop!" Aydin yelled, catching up to us.

"You found her?"

"Valencia's missing, and no word on Keller." Aydin stared at his phone.

"Let's go."

Aydin talked on the phone as we headed back outside to a slew of police officers.

"Did something happen?" Teddy asked, joining us.

I grabbed him by the throat and shoved him against the car. "Where did you go?"

"Sorry, man. I went to pick up some food. I thought she was still in the building." Teddy flinched when I balled my fist up.

"You're fired."

"Let him go, Bishop." Aydin stood next to me.

"He's right, Bishop. We need to get going, and he's not worth the hassle." Rye patted me on the back.

I released Teddy and followed Rye to the car, dialing Yanira's number again.

The thirty-minute drive turned into fifteen with a police escort to Keller's home. The gate opened for us to drive up and park.

Keller opened the door with his staff behind him. "What's the meaning of this visit, Bishop?"

"Where's Jet?"

"Who?"

My hands clenched into tight fists. "Don't pretend you don't know, motherfucker."

Keller pointed toward the door. "I want you off my property."

"Where's Yanira?"

Keller seethed. "I have no idea what you mean, Bishop. I fired you, and now I'm putting a restraining order on you."

"We need to spread out and search," Rye suggested.

"Do you have a basement?" Aydin asked.

"Even if I have a basement, it doesn't mean you have the right to search it."

"As the mayor, I would think you'd want to know if someone committed a murder on your property," Aydin challenged.

"Murder! What the hell are you talking about?"

"Valencia isn't your niece?

Keller looked away and cleared his throat. "What I do in my private life is my business." He straightened his jacket and walked over to his staff.

"Valencia informed Yanira about you being a deadbeat landlord. Did you know that?"

"That's a lie."

"Valencia's the source, and now Yanira is missing."

"My lawyer handled those accusations," Keller responded.

"Even if you get them pushed under the rug, I'll be on your ass, Keller. Step aside or get put down," I barked.

Keller's security guard stepped forward, and Keller stuck his hand out to hold him back. "I have nothing to hide, so go ahead and look around."

Aydin waved for the rest of the team to go around back. I pulled out my gun and ran up the stairs, down the hall to each room, and charged inside. Rye opened each closet, and nothing was found.

I blew out a frustrated breath. "He has to have more property."

"Will find her. Let's try downstairs." Rye left the room, and we sprinted down the stairs. Keller's home was over ten thousand square feet and two stories. We approached the back of the house that led to a basement. I put a finger to my lips to keep quiet and twisted the knob slowly.

My phone buzzed in my pocket, I pulled it out and lifted it to see Aydin's message.

Aydin: *A side entrance door is open.*

Me: *Coming down now.*

I shoved the phone back in my pocket and slowly crept down the stairs with my gun in hand. When Aydin came in from the other side, and we both relaxed.

"He's not here," Aydin said.

"Shit!"

"Like I said, you have the wrong house." Keller approached the basement stairs.

My patience with him was running thin. "You've saved Jet on numerous occasions. Why?"

"Jet's one of the mentees. He had a hard life growing up, and I helped him get to a better place."

"From his criminal record, he's dangerous and unhinged."

"With therapy, he's become a better person, and I had his records sealed."

"How much does he have on you?"

"Nothing."

"He cleans up your secrets, and you make sure he doesn't go back to jail," Rye said, and things started to make sense.

Keller started to turn and paused. "Leave, or I'll call my lawyer and have you thrown out."

Soaquan said, "He's right. We need to keep looking."

Keller wasn't about to turn Jet over that easily if he had him on his side to handle his problems.

I jumped in the car with Rye, and as we pulled away from Keller's property, something finally clicked in my head.

Chapter 14

Yanira

It felt like days had passed being in this room, my mind replayed every interaction over the past few weeks. I prayed my family would find peace after everything that happened. Sweat dripped down my forehead and myheart beat fast, as Jet stood over me with a knife as the door exploded inward. Bishop charged him, and they both fell to the ground. Rye ran toward me and checked me over.

I lifted my hands to show him the handcuffs. "Get me out of here!"

"Hold on, Yanira. I got you," Rye said.

"No! She needs to die!" Jet screamed.

Bishop punched him in the stomach. "Motherfucker!" He raised his gun and smashed it across Jet's head repeatedly.

"Bishop! He's going to kill him," I yelled at Rye.

"Bishop! He's down," Aydin shouted and grabbed Bishop by the shoulder to push him back.

Rye helped me up after getting the handcuffs off. I cried and ran into Bishop's arms, burying my face in his chest.

His arms tightened around me as he kissed my temple. "He's gone," Bishop soothed.

"He killed Valencia," I sobbed at her bloodied body on the ground.

"I know, baby."

"How did you find me?" I lifted my head to look at him.

"After I tried Keller's place and the office, I figured the next best place was your building."

"He was going to set me up," I muttered, and Bishop nodded.

"Jet is Keller's henchman, and if he killed you and Valencia to make it look like you did it, then all his problems would disappear," Rye explained.

I wiped tears from my cheeks. "But Valencia was the snitch."

"And she wanted money from Keller to go away, and he wasn't budging," Aydin explained.

It all started to make sense. "So Jet killed our editor to cover for Keller and Valencia

for trying to blackmail him," I concluded.

Rye monitored the scene, gesturing to the other men. "Jet would do anything for Keller."

"Keller needs to be locked up."

"Don't worry about him. You're safe now." Bishop kissed me on the forehead.

"I love you."

Bishop wrapped an arm around my shoulder and helped me out of the storage room of the building. I walked out to a barrage of police and ambulances and saw Owen directing the press to stay back.

"What about Campbell and Kristen?"

"They had nothing to do with Jet and Keller. They were only trying to get ahead," Bishop informed me.

The coroner removed Valencia's body.

"Yanira!"

I glanced to the right and saw Chanel with Maddux, as she tried to get through the roped-off section. "Chanel!"

Bishop released me, and I ran toward her.

"Oh, God! Are you alright?" Chanel hugged me tightly.

All I could do was nod and cry in her arms. "I will be."

"Bishop called me, and I knew something was wrong. Maddux tried to keep me calm, but I needed to be here," Chanel recalled.

"I have to call my family, but I just want to be alone with Bishop right now."

Chanel held a blanket around my shoulders. "It's crazy that Jet worked with you."

"Never figured he was the one responsible for these murders."

"Take your time and get checked out," Chanel stated.

I walked back over to Bishop as Aydin and talked to the police.

* * *

The time on the clock read six thirty. I cut the carrots and tossed them in the skillet on top of the stove.

Bishop moved slowly around the table and lifted my chin. He pressed a kiss on my lips and cheek and behind my ear. I turned and slid my arms around his back as he sucked and nibbled along my shoulder and cupped my breast.

"I missed you, Nira."

"I've been home for the past week."

"Still doesn't feel like long enough."

Once Keller was investigated by the police for his

involvement with Jet, they looked into more of his shady dealings, and he was removed from office. A month had passed since Jet kidnapped me, and I still had moments of anxiety and stress from the ordeal. Being back in my routine helped, but a few times, I'd needed to be away from everyone. Bishop had been supportive, and I appreciated him letting me heal at my own pace.

"Food is wasting, thought you were hungry," I reminded him.

"Not hungry for food."

I giggled and stepped back to stare at him. "You're home early from work. No cases today?"

Bishop dropped his hands from my waist, picked up the salad bowl, and placed it on the table. "Aydin said I needed to take a little vacation to control my temper."

I watched him plop down in the chair. I'd rearranged some of his furniture and moved a few of my things here. I planned to move out officially of my place when I got the courage to return to my building.

"Maybe a vacation is good."

He winked at me. "Maybe."

"You can be a little harsh, babe."

He glared at me.

"Do you not remember when we first met and how closed off you were?"

"That's different."

I planted a hand on my hip and titled my head. "How?"

He grabbed the plates while I set the food on the table and took a seat. "You made it difficult for me to do my job."

"I made it difficult? I recall you forcing me under twenty-four-hour protection."

"I recall you never letting me rest peacefully."

The chime of the doorbell interrupted us.

"Who did you invite over?" He stood from his seat.

"Chanel and Farrah."

"There goes my quiet evening of sleep and TV."

We laughed as I followed him to the front door to let them in. When he stepped to the side, all three of us shook our heads at him.

"You have him trained well," Farrah jested.

I clapped my hand over my mouth to hold in my giggle.

"Yeah, I *really* need a vacation," Bishop mumbled to himself.

I leaned forward to kiss him and then led the girls to the kitchen.

"Sit where you want," I directed.

Farrah sat next to me, and Chanel sat across from Bishop.

Farrah and Chanel filled me in on their life updates, and we all discussed how the guys pushed Bishop to take a vacation because he was wound too tight. The entire dinner felt like old times, and I was grateful to be with my friends and my new love.

Hours after they left, I showered, climbed into bed, and cuddled up to Bishop. "What are you thinking about?" I laid my leg across his.

"How I'm thankful to have you back."

I kissed his chest. "I never left."

He cupped my chin. "Jet almost took you away from me."

"That could never happen." These moments when we could be alone and just talk meant the most to me.

"Keller won't be able to hurt anyone else again."

"Good. I hope it exposes everything he did."

"We'll see. My priority is making sure you're safe for the rest of your life." He pushed me onto my back.

I smiled. "And how will you do that?"

"I have my ways, Nira." Bishop slipped his tongue in my mouth and wrapped his hand around my waist. He lingered over my body as the TV played in the background, and we made up for lost time.

Epilogue

Yanira

I wanted everything to be on time, but my friends and family had a bad habit of taking their sweet time to do anything. I was worried that today would fall apart before Bishop got to see it. He could be hard to please and hated being the center of attention, so this would be the first and last time I planned a surprise party for his birthday.

I'd rented the bar near the alley where we bumped into each other that first night. The place was closed to the public for the night, and we'd brought all his favorite foods, a DJ, and half of the guests included the guys he worked with, plus my brother.

"Yanira, where do you want these?" Chanel held the tray of red velvet cupcakes

I'd ordered from the local bakery near my apartment.

"Can you put them near the front of the buffet table?" I motioned to the food and desserts arranged on the table.

Chanel nodded and sauntered to the front entrance near the bar. Aydin should show up with Bishop—who thought it was just the guys hanging out tonight—soon. He'd wanted to go out with me to celebrate, but I'd lied and said I had to work.

Bria approached me. "The guys are five minutes away."

I rubbed my hands together, nervous he would hate the party.

"Stop worrying. You're going to bite your nails off." Bria nudged me.

I dropped my hands to my sides. "He hates surprises, and I lied about working late."

"When he sees this, you won't have anything to worry about."

The DJ turned the music down, and the lights dimmed as everybody got into position. I smiled when the door opened, and Bishop looked around with a hiked brow.

"Why is it so dark in here?" he asked as the lights came up.

"Surprise!" Our collective shouts surprised him and he jerked back in shock. I ran into his arms and kissed him, parting his lips with my tongue.

He gripped my waist. "What is all this?"

I pulled back and wiped the lipstick off his lips. "A surprise party for you."

"I thought you had to work."

The warmth of his hands sent goosebumps up my arms. "I lied." I leaned into his chest.

Bishop gazed at me like I was his world. "I see." He grinned and cupped my chin.

I gripped his hand and escorted him to the large poster at the entrance to show him the display of our best pictures together. Then I tugged him to the bar and grabbed him a beer.

"Happy Birthday, Bishop." Bria and Chanel walked over with their husbands.

Bishop hugged Bria, then Chanel.

"Are you hungry? I have all your favorites." I pointed to the steak, burgers, hot dogs, and potatoes.

"Not right now."

"This is your night, and I want you to enjoy yourself."

"Having you next to me is enough." He pressed a kiss to my forehead. His eyes shifted to the DJ and the people on the dance floor. "When did you have time to plan the party?" He turned me around to face him and wrapped his arms around my waist.

"While you were out working. I talked to the owner and the guys to get you here."

"Babe, you're the best."

"You give me a reason every time I look into your eyes."

"Maybe for your birthday, we can go on a trip?"

I shrugged. My birthday wasn't for another six months. "I need to put in the time off and give them a good reason."

Bishop's gaze was on me. "I have a good reason for a trip."

"What?" I arched my brow.

He reached a hand into his pocket and pulled out a black box.

"Bishop!" I gasped and covered my mouth with both hands as he dropped to one knee.

The music stopped, and all eyes were drawn to us.

"Yanira, after our first meeting, I didn't think I could resist you. I mean, you drove me crazy."

Everyone laughed.

"I promised to protect you, and I meant it, so will you do me the honor of becoming my wife?" Bishop held up the ring.

I nodded. "Yes, I'd love to marry you!"

Bishop slid the ring on my finger, then stood to hug me.

Everybody cheered and congratulated us on our engagement. Bria and Chanel gazed at the ring.

My mom squealed like a schoolgirl. "I'm so proud of you, Yanira!"

"Thank you. We need drinks." I glanced at the bar.

Bria handed us each a glass of champagne. "Try not to get too wasted. You'll hate yourself in the morning."

"Bishop is worth the risk." I winked at him and sipped on the champagne.

He nuzzled my neck. "Worth every battle."

* * *

I hope you enjoyed Yanira and Bishop's story, check out Kadence and Gunner in **Seek to Earn**: https://book s2read.com/u/bPgyRz

Don't forget, if you love bodyguard, forced proximity romance, check out **Protecting Chanel**: https://book s2read.com/u/mqwPB8

If you love brother's best friend romance, you'll love **Sensual:** https://books2read.com/u/49lYYM with a dash of steamy romance.

Check out this bodyguard, military romantic suspense **Protecting Bria:** https://books2read.com/u/bQJkjd

Another military romance suspense featuring familiar characters **Protecting Chanel**: https://books2read.com/ u/mqwPB8

How about a steamy, medical romance? Check out **Haven:** https://books2read.com/u/4jAvyZ for a steamy enemies-to-lovers romance.

Have you checked out **His Peace, Her Pleasure?** https://books2read.com/u/3JJroP for a billionaire, steamy romance.

Please also check out my **_Love Don't Live here Anymore:_** https://books2read.com/u/mBOWGZ for a steamy enemies-to-lovers romance.

About the Author

A TENNESSEE NATIVE and California dreaming Author, KeKe Renée, is living and striving to continue her passion for writing short story romances in genres ranging from Erotic, Paranormal, and Women's Fiction.

Coming Soon!

Tempt Me: Billionare Boy's Club Book 4
Ravafe Me:: Billionaire Boy's Club Book 5
TN Nashville Division Book 4
TN NAshville Division Book 5

What's Next?

Catalogue of Releases by Keke Renée:

•Wet Heat (Wet Heat Series Book 1)

•Every time We Touch Novelette (Wet Heat Book 2 Series)

•His Peace, Her Pleasure

•Baby, It's Cold Outside

•Love Don't Live Here Anymore, Vanessa Andrew Book 1

•Love Don't Live Here Anymore, Isabella Andrew Book 2

•One Night Only-A Novelette (Love By Design Book 1)

•Cassian and Savannah (Love By Design Book 2)

•Deidra's Love (Love By Design Book 3)

•Protecting Bria TN Seal Security Nashville Division Book 1

•Protecting Chanel TN Seal Security Nashville Division Book 2

•Protecting Yanira TN Seal Security Nashville Division Book 3

•Haven

•Taste (A New Adult romance)
•Sensual
•Seek To Please
•Seek To Bare
•Seek To Touch
•Seek To Love
•Seek To Trust
•Seek To Earn

Thank you so much for reading and if you enjoyed the crazy ride and decide to leave a review we'd truly appreciate the support.

Catalog of Releases By Chiquita Dennie

Series

<u>Struck in Love</u>

The Early Years-A Prequel Short Story

Ruthless:Antonio and Sabrina Book 1

Savage: Antonio and Sabrina Book 2

Beast: Antonio and Sabrina Book 3

Captivated By His Love:Janice and Carlo

Brutal: Antonio and Sabrina Booke 4

Redemption: Antonio and Sabrina Book 5

<u>Heart of Stone</u>

Broken, Book 1 (Emery & Jackson)

A Valentine's Day Short Book 1.5 Emery & Jackson

Rebirth, Book 2 (Jordan and Damon)

Reveal, Book 3 (Angela and Brent)

Bottoms Up Book 3.5 Jessica and Joseph Short

Renew, Book 4 (Jessica and Joseph)

<u>Cocky Billionaire Boys</u>

Cocky Catcher (Cocky Billionaire Boys Book 1)

Bossy Billionaire (Cocky Billionaire Boys Book 2)

<u>The Fuertes Cartel</u>

Stolen (The Fuertes Cartel Book 1)
Saved (The Fuertes Cartel Book 2)
Betrayed (The Fuertes Cartel Book 3)
<u>Carrington Cartel</u>
Torn: The Carrington Cartel Book 1
Claim: The Carrington Cartel Book 2
<u>Something</u>
Something Gained: A Romantic Comedy Book 1
Something Earned: A Romantic Comedy Book 2
<u>Pierce Motors</u>
Refuel: (Pierce Motors Book 1)
Pressure: Pierce Motors Book 2)
<u>Summer Break</u>
Summer Nights: (Summer Break Book 1)
<u>TN Seal Security</u>
Aydin: Book 1
Nasir: Book 2
Nicco: Book 3
<u>Standalones</u>
Until Serena(HEA World Novel)
Temptation
She's All I Need
I Deserve His Love
Mutual Agreement
Scoring with Sadie
Exposed (A Bodyguard Novel)
Love Shorts:A Collection of Short Stories
Red Light District(A Fantasy Romance Short)

Acknowledgments

I CAN'T MENTION ENOUGH the support and dedication of my author buddies for keeping me uplifted. My behind-the-scenes team to beta readers, editors, designers, and more. As a writer, I continue to strive for the best, and I appreciate everyone who reads my work. Without your continual feedback, I wouldn't be on this path, letting doubts slip away.

304 Publishing Company

WE SHOWCASE AUTHORS writing African American, Interracial, Women's Fiction, Urban Romance, Erotic, and Contemporary Romance novels. Along with Thriller, Suspense, Poetry, Beauty, and Style Books. Thank you for taking the time to visit. Join our mailing list to stay updated with new releases and blog posts.

www.ingramcontent.com/pod-product-compliance
Lightning Source LLC
Chambersburg PA
CBHW011141190726
48289CB00012B/3103